𝕷𝖔𝖓𝖌𝖇𝖔𝖚𝖗𝖓

Nickolae Gerstner

STARGAZER
Publishing Company
"Educate, Enlighten, Entertain"

Published by Stargazer Publishing Company
PO Box 77002
Corona, CA 92877-0100
(800) 606-7895 (Order line)
(951) 898-4619 (Main office)
FAX: (851-898-4633
Corporate e-mail: stargazer@stargazerpub.com
Orders e-mail: orders@stargazerpub.com
www.stargazerpub.com

Cover design by Michael Wheary

ISBN: 978-1-933277-09-7

LCCN: 2008926490

Acknowledgements

With gratitude to Carol J. Amato, Ruth Gerstner, Sandra Bates, the Writers' Club of Whittier, and—most especially—to Karen Kae Waldrip, my first and best critic.

Books by Nickolae Gerstner

Dark Veil

No Bed in Deseret

Books co-authored by
Nickolae Gerstner
and Barbara Pronin
writing as
Barbara Nickolae

Finder's Keepers

Ties That Bind

About *Longbourn*

"Lively characters, a convincing plot, and humor that would set Jane Austen laughing."

— *Madeline Baker, writer*

About *Dark Veil*

"*Dark Veil* takes exciting twists and will keep readers guessing until the last page. A great read."

— *Catherine Nelson, Rave Review*

About *No Bed in Deseret*

"…a good read that's also unconventional and moving."

— *West Coast Review of Books*

About *Ties That Bind*

"Readers who dive into this lively take may not want to resurface until the end."

— *Publisher's Weekly*

About *Finder's Keepers*
(also a *Reader's Digest* condensed book selection and translated into 14 languages)

"*Finder's Keepers* is my kind of book…a neat, suspenseful plot about the kind of people you worry about, written with skill."

— *Tony Hillerman*

"Emotionally gripping. I loved it from the first page."

— *Mary Higgins Clark*

"Nickolae's first novel displays ingenuity and daring…."

— *Publisher's Weekly*

"A nifty thrilled about a kidnapped child…a promising debut."

— *Kirkus Reviews*

"An unusually expert and clever work…plotting is ingenious, eminently readable and suspenseful."
— Charles Champlin, *Los Angeles Times*

"Well drawn and believable. A splendid find."

— *Baltimore Sun*

Dedicated to

Miss Elaine,
Miss Sarah, Miss Natalie,
Miss Kayla,
and, of course,
Miss Jane

Chapter 1

It is a truth universally acknowledged that a single man in possession of a good fortune must be in want of a wife.

This truth Mr. Algernon Bennet disdained when death rendered him single again after twenty-three years of exasperating marital bliss. Before the earth mounded over the first Mrs. Bennet, he knew there would never be a second.

His return to single life occurred when he was forty-four years of age. On an ordinary evening, his lady complained, first about her poor nerves, then about palpitations. Scarcely a day had ever faded without her describing her nerves. Algernon was so familiar with their adventures, he thought of them as the guests who never went home. The report on her palpitations was followed by an accounting of the day's grievances.

He recalled later that her litany had sounded no different than usual, and he had ignored her in rapt silence. At bedtime, he bade her a casual good night, lit his candle from hers, and went upstairs.

The next morning, he made his usual tramp of the grounds of Longbourn, his Hertfordshire estate. Though neither large nor grand enough to be called a noble estate, its farms and flocks secured two thousand pounds a year, enabling him to provide a comfortable home for his wife and five daughters.

The house was spacious, and Algernon never minded the peeling paint or walls with cracks inching larger every year. He thought it picturesque that the steeple on Longbourn church pointed decidedly toward the setting sun rather than the sun at midday. Longbourn was dear to him just as it was, and he enjoyed ambling through the flower garden, now in full summer bloom.

When he returned to the house, he went to the library and began sorting neglected correspondence. Hill knocked on the door. Before he could respond, she knocked again, loud and insistent.

"Mr. Bennet. Mr. Bennet."

"Come in, Hill."

She opened the door and stood motionless on the threshold, her hands clasped as if in prayer. She had been the housekeeper at Longbourn for fifteen years, and Algernon admired the adept way she soothed Mrs. Bennet's tirades. She never interfered during the first ravings, but when Mrs. Bennet was obliged to recover her breath, Hill would approach her with comforting gestures and calming words. Now she appeared to need comfort herself.

Algernon selected a letter to attend to. "Is something wrong, Hill?"

"Yes, Sir."

"With Mrs. Bennet, I suppose."

Hill's nod was very slow.

"What is it this time?" he asked, eager to have done with it.

"Sir, she is dead."

"Dead?" Algernon looked up. "What do you mean, Hill?"

"I mean, Sir, when Sarah brought Mistress her tea, she was very still and not alive."

Her jittery nerves and flutterings were all too familiar, but his wife had never appeared dead before. It was a new complaint, and a good whiff of smelling salts would undoubtedly set her right. He shrugged. "What am I to do about it?"

Hill started to cry. "The parson—you have to tell him. And Miss Mary. We have not told her. You had to be told first."

Algernon went rigid. When he could move, he tossed the letter, bolted from his chair, and ran up the stairs. Sarah, the cook, and the new housemaid stood at the foot of his wife's bed, weeping and staring at a face with closed eyes and a strangely benign smile.

"Lydia." Leaning over her, he called out her Christian name, something he had rarely ever done. They always addressed each other as Mr. and Mrs. Bennet. At this critical moment, a more intimate salutation seemed appropriate.

She did not answer his cry of Lydia, nor would she have responded to Mrs. Bennet. She was indeed dead. The shock to Algernon left him almost unable to draw breath. He stared at the fixed smile, remembering the beautiful Miss Gardiner who had been so cheerful and good-natured during their brief courtship. He touched her face, murmured her name again, and then, too stunned to think, too stunned to feel, stumbled into the hall.

Mary rushed toward him. "Papa, is it true? Is my dear mother dead?"

A nod was the only response Algernon could manage.

"Life is a gift that can be snatched away without warning." Mary's voice broke on a sob, but she persevered. "We must console each other and face this trial bravely."

Algernon stared at her, amazed that, even in this devastating moment, she spoke like a young lady devoted to copying lofty tracts from thick volumes.

Hill, the butler, and other servants gathered at the foot of the stairs, their hands folded, their eyes downcast. The sight of them forced Algernon to rally. "Mary, we must write to your sisters. Hill, please notify the parson and send for the surgeon."

Mary was his only daughter still at home. His youngest, Lydia Wickham, just like her mother in name, looks, and manner, was in Norfolk, where her husband had been transferred with the militia. Knowing neither of them ever had a farthing to spare, he included a bank note with her letter to pay for the trip home to bid farewell to her mother.

No bank notes were needed in the letters to his eldest daughters. Elizabeth's husband, Fitzwilliam Darcy, though untitled, was master of a huge estate and the richest man in Derbyshire. Jane, his first-born, was the happy and devoted wife of Charles Bingley, whose fortune exceeded five thousand pounds a year. Kitty, his fourth daughter, lived with the Bingleys.

Soon the surgeon arrived riding hard, a waste of exertion, as quicker attention could not benefit his patient. He spent time alone in her room and, when he emerged, gave his solemn pronouncement: "It is possible a rapid pestilence corrupted her breathing. However," he added, polishing his spectacles, "the bottle of sleeping draughts on her night table is almost empty. Her maid said she noticed it yesterday and is certain it was full. Perhaps Mrs. Bennet sadly forgot an earlier dose and ingested a second dose, bringing on this regrettable result."

Soon neighbors began calling to express their shock and offer condolences. When they made kind inquiries about how long she had been ill, Algernon had no answer, remembering he had ignored her complaints the night before. He felt a rush of guilt, but his temperament was such that guilt never held his attention for long. He forgave himself with the thought that, had he been more solicitous, the shock to Mrs. Bennet might well have abbreviated the few hours of life she had remaining.

By the time the neighbors had left and night had fallen, Algernon was recovered enough to know the business of death was being properly managed. He retreated to his library after telling Hill he was not to be disturbed. His sorrow craved solitude, a little brandy, and perhaps the solace of his new book.

Chapter 2

The first people to call the next day were Sir William and Lady Lucas, who had been the nearest neighbors to Longbourn for many years. Lady Lucas's handkerchief was constantly pressed to her face. She could hardly utter a word without spilling tears. She and Mrs. Bennet had enjoyed an intimate and tender friendship, the depth of which was exceeded only by their fierce rivalry and determination to outdo each other.

Early in their acquaintance, Algernon enjoyed many private laughs at the invariable silliness of Sir William and his lady, but their ability to entertain had wearied long ago. Joining them in the drawing room, he felt an unexpected tenderness. Seeing Lady Lucas's tears, he felt a rush of moisture to his own eyes.

When Sir William anxiously repeated his condolences, Algernon grasped his hand. "My dear
friend and neighbor, you must allow me to be of
service," Sir William said valiantly. "Name the task
you wish me to perform."

Sir William had amassed a comfortable fortune
in trade, and the dazzling event of his life was his
unexpected elevation to the knighthood. From the
moment he was first called Sir William, he had
desired nothing more than to be chivalrous and
benevolent to all. Algernon knew Sir William revel-
ed in being helpful and wished he could oblige.
Unfortunately, he could think of nothing for Sir
William to do.

When they were seated, Algernon noticed Lady
Lucas looking at him, not a cursory glance but
rather an intense stare. "Dear Mr. Bennet," she said,
breaking a long silence, "how do you feel?"

He had no quick answer. Surely, he was sad. His
wife had just died. He was shocked, too, but knew
the weight of what had happened had yet to settle
in. Finally, he said, "Thank you for your concern. I
am managing."

"Oh, Mr. Bennet, are you quite healthy?" She
still studied him closely, and Algernon thought he
detected something hopeful in her voice.

Before he could assure her that his health was
unimpaired, she said, "We are worried about you. It

is well known that one such sad event so often precedes another." Her mouth twitched. Despite her constant employment of a handkerchief, she was repressing a little smile. Algernon's brush with sentiment vanished.

In a self-assessment, he suspected he had more flaws than virtues. Consequently, self-assessment was something he never aspired to, but he took pride in having one superior ability. He was adept at reading people and understanding their motives. An astute observer, he was sometimes delighted and sometimes appalled when handsome reasons were claimed for self-serving behavior. However, no great skill was needed to understand Lady Lucas's sudden interest in his health. She was enjoying hopes Longbourn would not long be without a mistress, and the new mistress she had in mind was her daughter.

In default of a male heir in the direct Bennet line, Algernon's beloved Longbourn was entailed on a distant cousin, a clergyman named William Collins. When Mr. Collins heard about the charm and beauty of the Bennet daughters, he had traveled from his parish in Kent to visit Longbourn, intending to select a wife. He quickly singled out Elizabeth to be honored with his proposal and threw himself at her feet. He was indignant at her refusal, but he had come to Hertfordshire to find a wife and would not be thwarted.

Three days later, he threw himself again, this time at the feet of Elizabeth's best friend, Charlotte Lucas. A plain woman of twenty-seven, Charlotte had overlooked his being outstandingly disagreeable and accepted him to elude spinsterhood. She was now Mrs. Collins. If Algernon was gracious enough to make haste and join his wife in death, Lady Lucas's dear Charlotte would become the wife of a landed gentleman and a near neighbor.

Confident he understood the lady's interest in his longevity, Algernon wondered if it was too soon after his bereavement to be amused. He was about to entertain himself by assuring her that the men in his family were exceptionally long-lived when Mary joined them. She carried a crushed handkerchief in one hand, a large book in the other.

Lady Lucas embraced her. "My poor Mary."

"Sir William, Lady Lucas, now that the angel of death has cast his cloak over my dear mother, it is a comfort to have friends gather around us."

"Gather we shall," said Sir William, giving his head a noble tilt.

Lady Lucas dabbed at her eyes again. "I cannot believe it, such a terrible shock."

"From everything I have read," Mary said, "even when it is expected, the death of a dear one is a shock. When the death is unexpected, the shock is even more shocking."

Despite her best effort, Mary rarely made the scholarly impression she strived for, but it did not matter. She was never listened to. Lady Lucas had already turned her attention.

"Dear Mr. Bennet, when do you expect Mrs. Bingley and Mrs. Darcy?"

"Their letters were sent express and should have reached them by now. They are probably on the road. If the clear weather holds, they may get here sometime tomorrow."

Other neighbors arrived, anxious to take his hand and murmur words of sympathy. It was not quite the time for Algernon to recollect quarrelsome Mrs. Bennet, yet listening to praise of that blessed and wonderful woman, he found himself wondering who it was they had in mind.

A few days after attaining his majority, he had married, certain he was embarking on a life filled with domestic bliss. All too soon, he had realized bliss was out of the question. His wife's lovely face could not compensate for her being an unreasonable, complaining woman who was never content.

After his initial distress, Algernon abandoned futile regrets, accepted responsibility for his choice, and resolved to be amused by her behavior. Now he admitted that, for her sake and even more for their daughters, he should have strived to improve her conduct, even if her mind was beyond repair.

Listening to condolences, it struck him hard that he had not been a good husband. Fatherhood had been a failure, too. Elizabeth was his favorite, but he loved all his daughters. Their welfare had always been important to him, especially when promoting it did not cause him too much trouble.

The grief he felt over his wife's death was not as painful as acknowledging his poor performance as a husband and father. A thousand memories loomed of times when he should have done better. Ah, memories were too disagreeable. He would think about something else.

Chapter 3

Algernon thought he had been dreaming and stared at the ceiling as reality settled in. It had not been a dream. His wife was dead, and he was filled with regrets. Their marriage had not been happy, but there had been better moments. He was almost sure of it.

A carriage was approaching. Judging from the thunderous sound, it was pulled by a large team. He was certainly not able to deal with callers. They could present their cards and go away.

Someone was running up the stairs. "Father!"

Jumping out of bed, he pulled on his robe, opened the door, and held out his arms to Elizabeth. They had a long, silent embrace. She and her mother had rarely managed to be of like mind, but her red, swollen eyes spoke of sincere grief.

"Lizzy, I am so glad you are here."

"We were on the road in less than an hour after we got the terrible news. When we changed horses, Darcy hired their best team." She brushed a strand of hair off his forehead. "Oh, Father, such a terrible shock. Are you all right?"

He nodded but could not answer. He felt too strange, too bewildered, to know how he was.

"You have not had your tea. Do you want it up here?"

"Stay and have it with me if Darcy will not mind."

"He knows I want time alone with you, and his sister is with us. Georgiana was so concerned for me, she begged to come." Elizabeth hesitated. "I hope...I hope her coming to Longbourn will not create a problem."

Algernon shrugged. "What problem could there be?" Elizabeth rang the bell, and Algernon went into his dressing room to change. When he returned, Elizabeth was arranging tea on his little table. Sarah carried in a second chair.

"Sit down, Father," Elizabeth said, filling his cup. "I want you to tell me everything you can bear to talk about. Had my mother complained of being ill?"

Raising his eyebrows, Algernon looked at her.

Elizabeth understood. "Poor mother, there was rarely a day when she did not worry her nerves."

"The surgeon thinks she took a strong dose of her sleeping draughts, then accidentally took more." He sighed. "If that be the case, the efficacy of the draughts cannot be questioned." Suddenly, his voice was unsteady. "Lizzy, I should have paid more attention."

She grasped his hand. "Father, I am sure there was nothing you could have done."

His Lizzy had come and was consoling him. Algernon's spirits began to improve. "Your mother's death was certainly unexpected, and we must rejoice for her."

"Do you mean because it happened too quickly for her to have suffered?"

He shook his head. "When we finally abandoned hope of having an heir, your mother was afraid when I died, William Collins would throw her out of Longbourn to starve in the hedgerows. To console her, I promised to be the survivor." He paused. "I am not altogether certain she cherished that idea. However, now that I *have* outlived her, she is spared from worries about losing her home."

Even when it eluded everyone else, Elizabeth appreciated his wit, but she looked askance at this attempt. He tried again. "The last year of her life was probably the best. She was never happier than when she was boasting about Jane's rich conquest or telling how you ensnared Mr. Darcy."

"Papa! I am quite of the opinion he ensnared me." Her smile flickered. It was the best Algernon could hope for.

"Lizzy, when do you think the Bingleys and Kitty will get here?"

"I doubt Jane would spend the night jostling in a carriage with her confinement approaching. They probably stopped in an inn and will not get here before nightfall."

She refilled his cup. "Have you had time to think of what you are going to do for Mary?"

"Do for Mary," he repeated. "What do you mean?"

"I know after the four of us were gone, Mary spent a great deal of time with Mama. Poor Mary will feel all alone now."

Poor Mary indeed. She had always held a unique though unenviable position in his family. Elizabeth and Jane, his rational daughters, were devoted to each other. The wild two, Kitty and Lydia, paired off also. Mary had no partner, nor did she share in her sisters' beauty. The only plain one, she devoted herself to the pursuit of deep and devastating knowledge.

When Mrs. Bennet's other daughters left home, she had needed Mary, who became her companion both at Longbourn and on visits. Mary could philosophize after every morning call, and she seemed to enjoy being drawn into society. Their mother's death would bring a bigger change to her daily life than to the lives of her sisters.

When they finished their tea, Elizabeth went in search of Mary. Later, Algernon joined everyone downstairs. They did not hear him approach, and Algernon glimpsed Elizabeth standing with her head resting on Darcy's chest. His arms were around her, his face bent to hers.

Her voice was almost a whisper, but Algernon overheard: "Darcy, I know how concerned you are for Georgiana, but if he comes, I will—" Seeing her father, she broke off.

Darcy offered Algernon his hand. "Sir, I am sorry." He did not elaborate nor give way to dramatic expressions of grief. His expression and the sincerity of his words needed no enhancement.

"My sister is with us. I will call her."

"Here I am." Georgiana Darcy had entered the room too quietly to be heard. She gave Algernon a deep curtsy, then raised a tear-stained face. Her eyes were swollen. Surely, she had spent as much time in tears as Elizabeth, and she would have been crying *for* Elizabeth. Her acquaintance with Mrs. Bennet was scant, but she loved her sister-in-law. Her own parents had been many years dead, and Elizabeth's early letters as Mrs. Darcy had frequent mention of Georgiana's growing affection and eagerness to be loved. To Algernon, someone's loving Elizabeth needed no explanation and enhanced his opinion of her young sister-in-law.

The stream of neighbors and friends began early and endured through the day. Elizabeth remained at his side and, when the door closed behind the last caller, she took a place at the window, peering into the deepening night. Her husband stood behind her, his hands resting protectively on her shoulders.

On first acquaintance, Algernon had viewed Darcy as cold-hearted and very proud. He had been horrified when Elizabeth accepted his proposal and had begged her to reconsider. At her insistence, he got to know Darcy better and found, hidden behind his reserve, a man far more amiable than casual encounters could detect. Eventually, Algernon took pleasure in their match, not because of Darcy's great fortune and devotion to Elizabeth, but because he was convinced Elizabeth loved him.

Her influence on him was evident. The man no longer behaved as if serious was the only acceptable demeanor. It had amazed and delighted Algernon when he observed that far from objecting to Elizabeth's playful teasing, Darcy relished it. His dignity was unimpaired, but he had learned to appreciate jokes at his own expense. Seeing them in comfortable intimacy, Algernon wondered if his convictions of a lifetime might be wrong. Perhaps it was possible, however rare, for a man and woman to be happily married.

He was weary but would not go to bed until the others had retired, and Elizabeth still hoped the Bingleys would arrive. Algernon was about to say there was little chance of it when a carriage sounded in the distance.

Elizabeth cried out, "Here they are!"

Mary hastened downstairs, and they gathered to welcome Jane, Kitty, and Bingley with embraces, kisses, and tears. Only Lydia and Wickham were missing to complete the family.

Although approaching motherhood rounded her figure and beautiful face, Jane's sweet smile was untouched. "Dearest Papa," she said, moving into his arms and kissing him.

Charles Bingley had easy, pleasant manners, and Algernon had occasionally wondered how such an intelligent a man could be so good-natured. To everyone who knew them, he and Jane were considered a perfectly matched couple. Even now, as he offered his regrets and concern to Algernon, he kept a supportive arm around his wife.

Wickham was a scoundrel, but Algernon had two daughters who had been clever enough to fall in love with excellent men who were themselves clever enough to have inherited fortunes. It relieved Algernon to know that even though he could not leave his daughters an inheritance, the two eldest were rich and would make sure their younger sisters were never in want.

When she said goodnight, Elizabeth slipped her arm through Algernon's. "Father, when Darcy and I return to Pemberley, we hope you and Mary will accompany us."

"Pemberley." He said it slowly, as if giving it consideration. He was not.

Chapter 4

The family waited for Lydia to arrive, one sister or another often at a window, staring down the lane in the hope of seeing her carriage. When Elizabeth stood sentry, Georgiana was always at her side. Seeing them together, Algernon was surprised to realize Georgiana was markedly the taller. Her demure, retiring manner robbed her impression of several inches. With Longbourn in mourning, her silence was understandable, but Algernon had yet to hear her say five words together.

When the old hall clock struck three, they could wait no longer. It was time. Algernon and the other men carried Mrs. Bennet out of the house forever. Georgiana joined the four sisters, and they pressed close to the windows to watch the sad procession make its way to the churchyard. Rain threatened, the dark cloud cover providing a suitably gray atmosphere.

Afterward, friends and neighbors called, looking properly sad and speaking in hushed tones. The Bingleys and, more especially, the Darcys received the most attention. Algernon endured expressions of sympathy by observing that condolences were doled out in surprisingly similar proportion to the wealth of the recipient.

Finally, the last carriage left. The family was alone and while they were at supper, a letter came. Algernon handed it to Jane to read aloud:

My dearest father, I cannot believe I will never see my dear mother again. I cried all night. Wickham had a problem with his colonel and was denied permission to leave his post, so we cannot...."

Algernon heard Darcy's sharp intake of breath and saw him and his wife exchange a telling look. "I am sorry about Lydia, but I told you *he* would not come," she whispered.

Theirs was not the only reaction. Georgiana's face reddened and she stared at her plate.

Remembering the exchange he overheard the previous day, Algernon realized they had been talking about Wickham. He never pried into other people's business, but this situation aroused his curiosity. Wickham had grown up at Pemberley and was the late Mr. Darcy's godson. His father had been steward to that great estate. Wickham and Darcy had been playmates and fellow students, but something had ruined their relationship. Elizabeth had told him Darcy and Wickham preferred to avoid each other. Algernon now suspected their breach in friendship had, in some way, involved Georgiana.

Jane's voice trailed. "My poor sister. The rest of her letter is so smeared and blotched, I cannot make it out."

"The writing is probably smeared because Lydia was crying. Tears can play havoc with ink. We read in Shakespeare—"

"Yes, Mary," Algernon said, interrupting. They did not need to hear a weighty excerpt from the Bard.

Lydia was her mother's favorite and pampered child. Even though careless in her regard for others, she had to feel the loss of her greatest supporter. Algernon was sorry she would not have the comfort of her family, and he could not help noticing she had not returned the banknote sent for her travel expenses.

When the funeral was over, Algernon planned to take pleasure and solace in the company of his two eldest daughters, but the Bingleys could stay only a week. Jane's confinement was drawing near. She had to get home, and it was foregone Kitty would go with her.

On her recent trips to Longbourn, Algernon had noted improvement in Kitty's behavior. In the past, she had been a shadow to Lydia and, although never equaling Lydia's loud and boisterous behavior, she had fretted away her time and followed wherever Lydia led. Now, at seventeen and still impressionable, she had Jane's gentle guidance and Elizabeth's influence also. The Bingleys had recently purchased an estate only thirty miles from Pemberley, and it pleased Algernon to know three of his daughters were in easy distance of one another.

The next morning, Georgiana's waiting-woman, a Mrs. Annesley, arrived from Pemberley. After she had rested a day from that journey, she set out with Georgiana who had a long-scheduled visit with her aunt, Lady Catherine de Bough, whose estate was in Kent.

Georgiana seemed reluctant to leave and clung to Elizabeth when they kissed goodbye. "It has been less than a year, yet in my heart, you have always been my sister. I will miss you very much and write every day."

It was the longest speech Algernon had ever heard her make. It sounded plaintive. Despite her wealth and cadre of servants, she knew what it was to be lonely. When she curtsied to him, he felt compelled to say, "I hope you will visit us again under happier circumstances."

The Darcys remained nearly a month, and one morning, when the family was in the sitting room, Sir William and Lady Lucas were announced. Lady Lucas began expressing her worries about Algernon as soon as the salutations were gotten through and she was seated.

"My dear Mrs. Darcy, I have already warned your father to be careful of his health. See how pale he looks?"

"Lady Lucas, my father has been out in the sun and looks rather burned."

Lady Lucas nodded as if Elizabeth had agreed with her. "I am afraid a man never does well after his wife is laid to rest."

"True, and the wish is never father to the thought," Elizabeth said, exchanging a glance with Algernon.

"Indeed, I hope my worries do not alarm you."

"To the contrary, Lady Lucas. I take your words as good counsel. If being without a wife shortens a man's time on earth, perhaps I should make haste and marry again. However, I had best wait until the black ribbons come off my sleeve."

"Papa!" Elizabeth sounded shocked, but she was fighting a smile.

"Marry again?" Lady Lucas said softly.

Algernon adjusted his cravat and tried to look as if he were evaluating his appearance as a future suitor. He ran his hand over his hair. It was still thick, although the screaming red of his youth had faded to a quiet auburn. "My dear Lady Lucas," he said, relishing the moment, "when the time is appropriate, I hope you will be kind enough to canvas the neighborhood and acquaint me with suitable ladies."

Sir William brightened: "Perhaps ladies who have been presented at court."

Algernon glanced at Darcy to see if he looked aghast at a conversation about a second Mrs. Bennet when the flowers on the grave of the first were still fragrant. His son-in-law sat nearby reading and never looked up. He was either indifferent or not listening.

Algernon pressed on. Smiling, he said, "Lady Lucas, I had been feeling poorly, but it does me a great benefit to realize I have two such considerate friends. I would not be surprised if you were already searching for my future wife."

With Elizabeth there, it was twice the fun to distress his considerate friend with talk of a marriage she clearly feared might prolong his life and delay her son-in-law's inheritance. Of course, she was dead wrong. The single life was going to agree with him. Marriage, on the other hand, had been a trial that, had he paid it more attention, might well have shortened his life.

After the Lucases left, Algernon and Elizabeth strolled the garden, enjoying the foliage of summer's finale. When Elizabeth mentioned something she wanted him to see at Pemberley, he decided it was time to let her know he was not going home with them. "Lizzy," he said gravely, "how do you think it would look if I went visiting so soon after your mother's death?"

"Father, I have never known you to be unduly concerned about what people think. As for visiting us, we are in mourning, too. We will not be entertaining."

"My dear, do you think it would be all right?"

"Of course, I think it would be all right. So do you. You are teasing me," Elizabeth said, smiling. "You and Mary have to come. If she is reluctant to leave home, I will tempt her with descriptions of the huge library at Pemberley."

"More books to copy impressive passages from. Exactly what your sister needs."

The day before Darcy was to leave for Pemberley, he joined Algernon in the library. Algernon stood at the window, and the two men gazed at a villager's passing hay wagon and to the stately trees and rolling hills beyond.

"Mr. Bennet, Elizabeth and I will be pleased to have your company, but be assured at Pemberley, you can have all the privacy you want."

His son-in-law had turned out to be a rational fellow with good character and sound judgment. While happy for Elizabeth's sake, Algernon rather regretted nothing about him provoked amusement.

When Darcy pressed him about visiting Pemberley, Algernon said, "I am giving the matter my sincere consideration and perhaps...." He stopped. Although tall himself, he was shorter than Darcy and felt shorter still in the man's imposing presence. This was not a man to trifle with. "I have no intention of leaving home," he said, "but I want Mary to go. Elizabeth and the maid are upstairs helping her pack."

"Yes, Sir," Darcy said, clearly respecting that Algernon had made up his mind.

Algernon and Mrs. Bennet had paid the required visit to Pemberley after Elizabeth and Darcy's marriage. Someday, when he was missing his favorite daughter, he would no doubt make a return visit. Now was not the time. Although he truly regretted his wife's death, regretted he had not better played his role as husband, he was eager to enjoy Longbourn with no tirades, complaints, and frisky nerves to keep him company.

Chapter 5

Although Algernon usually ignored female fashions, it pleased him to observe his daughter's quiet elegance. Elizabeth could have bedecked herself in feathers and lace abundant enough to display her importance and wealth as Mrs. Fitzwilliam Darcy. Instead, she remained unpretentious and, on the morning she, Darcy and Mary were to leave for Pemberley, she wore a simple green traveling dress. Her hair was glossy and dark, her eyes a deep brown, coloring inherited from her mother. Her great intelligence, wit and discernment were, of course, inherited from him.

On her left arm was a band of black ribbons. His own ribbon was on his right arm. He had lost a spouse, and his time of mourning would properly be longer, though it did not matter. It was unlikely he would want to do anything frowned on for a person in mourning. If he did, the ribbons on his arm would not discourage him.

After breakfast, he followed Elizabeth, Darcy and Mary outside where they stood on the damp lawn, saying their last goodbyes and watching the coachmen load the trunks onto the carriage. While sorry Elizabeth was leaving, he found it pleasant to contemplate having the house to himself. He missed his wife and found the sensation comparable to removing tight shoes. Something was different, but he could not complain.

Suddenly, Mary cried out. "Do not load my trunk!" She flung herself into Algernon's arms. "Dear Papa, the beloved companion of your life has been taken. I cannot abandon you to loneliness."

He was amazed that she thought her parents had been loving companions. Most of the time the relationship had resembled an armed truce—Bonaparte and Wellington taking tea together at Waterloo. He stifled a cough. "My dear," he said, patting her shoulder.

"Dear Papa, I will not—"

"Mary! Father will be fine," Elizabeth said. "I am sure he wants you to go."

"I do, indeed. You should—you *must* go."

Mary pulled off her bonnet, underscoring her determination to stay home. In the sunlight, her hair blazed as bright as Algernon's once had. His only red-haired daughter, she also had his love of books. However, he had never pursued knowledge as an adornment.

"Mary," Darcy said, "I hope when we get to Pemberley, you will kindly inspect our library and let us know if we are missing any volumes you think we should have." Although he spoke with his usual seriousness, Algernon caught his glance at his wife.

For a moment, it looked as if Darcy's tactic had worked. Mary wavered, then gave her head a violent shake. "My joy is in doing my duty, and my sacrifice is easily borne."

They took turns arguing with her and cajoling, and finally had to abandon the effort. She could not be persuaded. When the coachman cracked his whip to the horses, Mary stood at her father's side, one arm linked through his, the other waving farewell to her sister and brother-in-law.

Algernon walked into the house with Mary close beside him. He suspected she had lately been studying Joan of Arc. Still, he could not help being touched by her determination to stay with him. Touched indeed he was, though not pleased. Without her mother to draw her into company, she would be quite alone, except for him. The thought made him vaguely uneasy. It took only a few days for his unease to give way to distress.

The morning after the Darcys left, Algernon found Mary waiting at the door when he left for his morning walk. Smiling and eager, she fell into step with him. If she could keep up, he did not mind her company. Although she talked, he felt no obligation to listen. He quickened his already lively pace, and she went silent when she needed all her breath to keep up.

Mary waited for him the next morning and the next. She took breakfast with him and dinner. Her companionship was never mute, and she delighted in reading him impressive passages she copied from her favorite books. Her constant presence became more constricting than tight shoes.

One day, he had had quite enough and told Hill to serve his dinner in his library. Mary was hanging close by as usual and overheard.

"Dear Papa, you should not eat alone. I will have my dinner in the library, too."

"No," he blurted. "I do not want company."

Mary's smile crumbled, and she looked stricken. She had to know the library was his private domain, but Algernon regretted his harshness. He planned to praise her when she came up with a saying suitable for the occasion, but all she said was, "I am sorry, Papa." Turning, she went upstairs.

The next morning, she was not waiting when Algernon left for his walk. He did not see her until dinner, and then she was silent. Although he did not want her always hovering, he had not meant to crush her spirit and almost felt guilty. It was time for a little ingenuity.

"The house is too quiet," he said, signaling the butler to serve him more mutton. "It would be very pleasant if you could spend more time singing and practicing the pianoforte. We cannot have too much excellent music."

Mary was always eager to display her musical talents, such as they were, and looked delighted. Immediately after dinner, she hurried to open the pianoforte.

She was tolerably accomplished as a pianist, but her voice was weak, her manner pedantic. Algernon followed her to the instrument and loudly applauded her first song, then told her he could listen better from his library. "Keep playing. Keep playing," he insisted. With the library door closed, he rarely heard anything other than an occasional struggle with high notes.

Mary increased her hours of daily practice and badgered him about which were his favorite songs.

"Lullabies," he told her.

Mary could spend only part of each day singing lullabies. She still spent time trying to compensate for the loss of his beloved companion. He realized, far more than he wanted to, her excessive attentions were the acts of a lonely girl, distressed over the loss of her mother, who wanted attention from him. Again, the specter of his inadequacy as a parent rose to haunt him. Again, he sent it on its way.

On Sunday evening, he sat at his desk, absent-mindedly sketching the large oak tree outside the window. Suddenly, the solution occurred to him. It was incredibly simple. He would go to Pemberley and take Mary with him. After a brief visit, he would realize something at Longbourn required his attention. Quickly, he would order a carriage and be gone. Mary would remain at Pemberley to finish an extended visit. If Algernon had not been holding a pen, he would have rubbed his hands together.

Chapter 6

After his morning walk, Algernon hurried to the house, determined to be well on the way to Pemberley before midday. Summoning Hill, he told her to pack his trunk. Then he decided he had best mention it to Mary.

She was already thumping away on the pianoforte and finding her only required following the sound.

"My dear," he said, after an impatient wait for her to finish a piece, "that was excellent. Now get the maid to help you pack your trunk. We leave for Pemberley within the hour."

Mary looked up, bewildered. "Did an express come? Is something wrong?"

"Not at all. I just think it is time to visit your sister." A virtuous idea flashed. "Mary, I am happy you did not go to Pemberley with Elizabeth. Now I will have your company on the trip."

Mary blushed. "Thank you, Papa." Smiling, she dashed upstairs.

Algernon smiled, too, pleased with his thoughtfulness.

After giving instructions to Hill and his steward, he sent for a hired carriage, preferring to change horses on the journey rather than stopping to rest his own. When the carriage arrived from the village stable, he took his place. A breathless Mary joined him, and he rapped on the roof to signal the coachman to be off. It was a clear day, and they traveled the first miles in pleasant silence. Perhaps he had rushed her a bit, but soon she recaptured her breath and began commenting on the scenery.

Helpful though she was, Algernon did not need her to tell him the early turnings of autumn created a beautiful palette. He had a taste for color. As a youth, he had fancied himself an artist until he abandoned serious art forever after an oil painting he was especially proud of drew mortifying snickers when displayed in a private gallery. He still filled sketchpad after sketchpad with drawings of landscapes, animals, flowers—almost anything was a possible subject—but his drawings were private. He did not want critiques of his work and, whenever he had found his wife or a daughter snooping, he shouted her away.

"Papa, look," Mary said. "Look at that, too!"

"Yes, Mary," he said, already weary. Pemberley was a long way off. There would be many things she would be kind enough to point out.

They spent the night in an inn and were on the road again before first light. The sun was high when they reached the Pemberley woods. They traveled the estate's extensive grounds nearly a half-hour before reaching the house, a palatial structure beautifully situated on a rise of ground beside a lake. The great entry hall where they were received was lit by a chandelier adorned with slender, drop crystals sparkling in the light of many candles.

Algernon looked forward to Elizabeth's surprise and was not disappointed.

"Father!" The butler had scarcely enough time to announce them when Elizabeth, light on her feet and laughing, ran into the entry hall and into Algernon's arms. "It is just like you not to let us know you were coming."

She hugged her sister. "Dear Mary, I am delighted to have you."

Mary did not return her sister's hug. This was her first trip to Pemberley. She stood rigid, mouth open and speechless, staring at her surroundings.

As Mary gaped, Algernon said, "Elizabeth, I think your sister appears to be overcome. Perhaps she expected Pemberley to be more impressive and is disappointed."

"Our home is humble to be sure, but Darcy and I manage."

She issued instructions to the housekeeper to accommodate her father and sister in two of the best guest rooms and, slipping her arm through Algernon's, led him and Mary to a small sitting room decorated in a palate of pale colors. He had not seen the room on his earlier visit and suspected she had chosen it thinking Mary would regain her wits quicker in simple surroundings.

"Father, earlier I sent a carriage for a young man and his sister who live in Lambton. They will join us at dinner. Their mother also died recently, and she was a particular friend of Aunt Gardiner."

After traveling for hours, Algernon was not in the mood to be agreeable to strangers. He considered requesting a tray in his room but was torn by a desire for Elizabeth's company.

She seemed to interpret his hesitation. "You and Mary have been traveling and are probably tired, but please know I would love to have you at table."

He nodded. Her company was worth the effort.

"Darcy is out shooting with his cousin. You remember Colonel Fitzwilliam, do you not? He and the Peppers will be our only guests."

"The Peppers?" Algernon asked.

"The young man and his sister. They are Andrew and Dorinda Pepper."

"We share a common grief in the lost of a beloved parent," Mary said, coming to life. "I look forward to meeting them."

Because Elizabeth had invited them, the Peppers were not apt to be pompous or absurd, but Algernon hoped they would have some entertainment value. Perhaps she did not know them well, and they would expose themselves properly at dinner. Then he could have the pleasure of exchanging knowing looks with his Lizzy.

On Algernon's previous visit to Pemberley, he had left the joy of touring the house to Mrs. Bennet. She had thrilled to the importance and elegance of her second daughter's new home. When they returned to Longbourn, she had never stopped describing it to anyone who would listen for a second, third or tenth time. Algernon had preferred to stay in his quarters or wander the narrow lanes leading through the more secluded grounds of the vast estate. He had liked the family dining room better than the formal dining salon and had not been interested in the rest of the house. Without Mrs. Bennet at his side going into noisy raptures about everything, he now enjoyed his own tour after dressing for dinner.

When he climbed a flight of stairs to an upper floor, a massive clock immediately caught his attention. The detailed and asymmetrical carving on the dark wood case portrayed a stag, doe, peasants, and other wild game, indicating the clock was a German creation.

Beyond the clock was a long gallery, and the interior wall was lined with portraits of Darcy's family, most done by masters, and going back to the generations when the family name was D'Arcy. As Mrs. Bennet had described countless times, the portraits were framed in gold. The exterior wall of the room was lined with satin-draped windows that opened onto stunning views of a rock-dotted stream meandering among an array of stately trees. Studying the scene, Algernon selected several angles that provided worthy challenges for his sketching. The view he most favored was two trees, an oak and a Spanish chestnut, whose boughs tangled with each other above the stream.

Algernon stopped in front of a large portrait of Darcy, admiring the way the artist had captured a warm expression, especially in the eyes. At one time, Algernon would not have thought it a good likeness. Now he had to admit Darcy lived up to the good humor displayed in his portrait. Studying the fine brushwork, he was impressed, and he wondered how the artist had achieved the subtle blending of colors in the background.

He heard Mary and, turning, saw her with the housekeeper, whose name if he remembered right was Mrs. Reynolds, and another woman.

"Our outward beauty can be caught on canvas and serves our vanity," Mary said, waving her arm to indicate the portraits. "Our inner beauty is known only to those dear to us and God. I read that in Fordyce's sermons, and I think it is true."

The other woman nodded.

"Father, is that you?" Mary exclaimed.

"No, my dear. I assure you I am someone else," Algernon said, adhering to his custom of never respecting witless questions.

Mary did not seem to notice. "Father, let me introduce a new acquaintance. This is Miss Pepper. My father, Mr. Bennet."

Miss Pepper curtsied to him. "Mr. Bennet, I am honored to make your acquaintance, even if you are someone else."

Startled, Algernon gave her an appraising look. She had surely celebrated, or more likely regretted, her thirtieth birthday; she was tall, rather thin, and had unremarkable features.

The massive clock played a beautiful carillon, then struck the hour.

Mrs. Reynolds said, "Sir, if you please, it is time for you to go downstairs."

Algernon fell into step behind the ladies. Mrs. Reynolds led them to the drawing room and Darcy gave him an enthusiastic greeting. Georgiana also acted genuinely pleased to see them. At Longbourn, Elizabeth had told Algernon she was shy, an assessment even a brief observation confirmed. Anyone who called her a beauty would likely be considering her situation in life more than her face which was rendered pleasing more by a sweet expression than by handsome features. She immediately invited Mary to go riding with her in the morning, but Mary had to decline. She had never abandoned her studies long enough to become a horsewoman.

After shaking hands with Colonel Fitzwilliam, Algernon was introduced to Andrew Pepper, a man of about two or three and twenty, considerably younger than his sister. He was tall, and the coat he wore appeared to have been cut for a larger man.

Algernon was invited to escort Elizabeth and lead the procession into dinner. When they assembled, she took his arm.

"Father," she whispered, "I am delighted to see you, but I feel you have something devious in mind."

"You think your father devious?" He sounded indignant but was proud of her perception. Her talent for reading people was almost as good as his.

Darcy offered Mary his arm; the colonel and Miss Darcy were next, the Peppers last.

Mrs. Bennet had boasted about the Darcys having not one, but two French cooks. Algernon was certain that if they had only one cook, French or otherwise, it was enough. The dinner was superb and included apricot stuffed duck, his favorite. He was certain that after his arrival, Elizabeth issued orders for it to be served.

During dinner, a general conversation failed to develop. Algernon answered Elizabeth's queries about her Longbourn friends. Darcy talked to Mr. Pepper; the colonel attended to Georgiana, and Miss Pepper listened to Mary.

After the men were left to their port, Algernon picked up the gist of Darcy's conversation with Mr. Pepper. The young man was apparently wavering about whether he wanted to join the Royal Navy, and Darcy was encouraging him and offering to use his influence to help him obtain a commission.

Joining the ladies, Algernon noticed that Miss Pepper was still giving Mary rapt attention. He was intrigued. A person who could be fascinated by Mary had to be an amusing study.

When Mary took her coffee cup to the table, he approached Miss Pepper and made a small bow. "You and my daughter find a great deal to talk about. I daresay you find her conversation stimulating."

Miss Pepper stared at him with clear, gray eyes. "I enjoy our conversation. If I may say so, Miss Bennet seems eager to have someone to talk to."

It was ridiculous for him to feel uncomfortable. If Mary was lonely, it was neither his fault nor Miss Pepper's concern. For the second time, this woman startled him, and now he understood her silly response when they were introduced. She was one of those people who fancied themselves more intelligent than their fellows. It was an affectation he detested. He bowed again and turned away. There could be no amusement in talking to Miss Pepper.

Chapter 7

lgernon found Elizabeth waiting for him in the breakfast salon, and they enjoyed a private conversation. "Father," she began, pouring his tea, "the moment Jane's confinement starts, they will send word. Darcy has a carriage at the ready, and I will leave at once."

This was the opportunity he needed. "My dear, when you leave, it will be best for me to return to Longbourn, but we must not deprive Mary of a good, long visit. It would be cruel to tear her away before she has had time to read all the books in the great Pemberley library."

"*All* the books, Father?" Elizabeth said, giving him a knowing look. "She will always be welcome, and you must stay until it is time for you to go to the Bingleys to meet your first grandchild."

"My first grandchild," Algernon mused.

"If it is a boy, they will name him Bennet."

Bennet Bingley, Algernon thought, not impressed with the name. Of course, he had never liked the name Algernon, either.

"A grandson would be a nice change after five daughters."

He shrugged. "A grandson cannot change the entail. Longbourn will still go to Mr. Collins. A worthier hypocrite the world has seldom seen."

"He is an oddity, and Mother detested him for being the heir, but that is not something he accomplished on his own. The Peppers are in a similar situation."

"Do you mean Mr. Pepper is going to inherit an estate, because a man somewhere could not manage to father a son?"

Elizabeth shook her head. "Their mother had a lifetime interest in their stepfather's estate. When she died, the estate went to his nephew. Now they have only a small income and live in a cottage on the grounds."

Elizabeth encouraged her father to try the plum sauce and clotted cream with his scone. "Mr. Pepper needs a career. He favors the navy but is reluctant to accept Darcy's offer of help, because he does not want to leave his sister alone."

"Speaking of oddities, she has merit in that direction."

"Not at all! I met her when she and her mother visited Aunt Gardiner here. I like her and think you would, too, if you knew her better."

"Lizzy, perhaps I misjudged her," Algernon said, confident he had not. Elizabeth had perception, but her insight could not be expected to equal his. Occasionally, she was wrong.

After breakfast, Algernon treated himself to a long walk. He noted his bearings, planning to take a different path on his next outing. He could never cover all of Pemberley, but the variety of foliage and windings was great, and he planned to explore as many aspects as possible.

Later, Algernon went to the library and entered through ornately carved and gilded double doors. He read history and essays with pleasure, but neither genre delighted him as much as a good novel. Perhaps the latest work of Walter Scott had been added to the collection. He was inspecting a shelf of new volumes when he heard voices.

"The shop in Lambton has a large selection of muslins at good prices. Last week, a friend bought a beautiful paisley for three shillings a yard."

"Oh, I would like a new dress, but I wonder if it would be all right. I am still in mourning."

"I am sure your dear mother would want you to have a new dress. With your pretty red hair, you should try blue or perhaps green."

The library was L-shaped. Algernon was in one section, the ladies in the other. Tall bookcases were in-between. He remained quiet, hearing feminine chatter about bonnets, muslins, and the latest styles. He did not need the mention of red hair to recognize Mary's voice but pondered the other lady's identity.

"Miss Bennet, I am happy to help, but there is nothing to do. This library has every book I ever heard of."

"I think Mr. Darcy asked me to check his library to persuade me to come to Pemberley."

It was the sanest thing Algernon had ever heard Mary say. She was chatting cheerfully and not trying to impress her companion with the height and weight of her knowledge. Curious, Algernon peeked to see who had evoked such an unnatural response from his middle daughter and was seen himself.

Curtsying, Miss Pepper said, "Mr. Bennet, I trust this time it is you."

He responded with a slight bow, unimpressed with her attempt at wit.

"She came to help me, but we are not getting much done," Mary said, smiling.

Miss Pepper pointed to a small table clock encased in silver filigree. "I think it is time for me to go home."

"I will go with you. We will tell the coachman to go slow, so we can have a nice, long ride."

Mary had just made the tedious journey from Longbourn. If she wanted another carriage ride, it was for Miss Pepper's company. It pleased him to know Mary had found someone as silly as she was and had made a friend.

That evening, while waiting for dinner to be announced, Algernon noticed how attentive Colonel Fitzwilliam was to Miss Darcy. The colonel was the second son of an earl, and apparently the heir was unnecessarily healthy and unlikely to relinquish his position through demise. Elizabeth had once confided to Algernon that in the early days of their acquaintance, she had caught the colonel's eye. He had closed it when he found out she was without fortune. His behavior to Miss Darcy could be testing whether the right lady of fortune might be his own ward. Algernon had been told that since the death of the young lady's parents, the colonel had been joined with her brother in Georgiana's guardianship.

At seventeen, Miss Darcy was without the proud, almost arrogant, manner that formerly characterized her brother. Instead, she seemed eager to be liked and always referred to Elizabeth as "my dear sister." Her appreciation of his favorite raised her in Algernon's esteem.

Once or twice, he looked at Elizabeth, wondering if she thought the colonel was displaying his courting colors, but she was busy teasing Darcy. The two were laughing and remained absorbed with each other until they all assembled to go into the dining salon.

The last course had just been served, the last wine glasses filled, when the butler entered and held a silver salver out to Darcy. "Sir, this express just arrived."

Jumping up, Elizabeth rushed the length of the table and snatched the letter before Darcy could take it. "It is from Bingley. Jane's confinement has started. I will leave immediately and—" She stopped. "It is not from Bingley. Father, it is for you, from Lydia."

An express from Lydia could not bring good news. Algernon took a sip of wine, composing himself, then rose from his chair and took the letter from Elizabeth. "Let us see what your youngest sister has to say," he said, sounding more cheerful than he felt.

Dearest Father, I am in terrible trouble and I beg you to help me. Wickham owed money. They were going to put him in prison. I was afraid for him and paid his debt with a bank check. I thought it would soon be good. I did not know we had already spent Wickham's monthly stipend. Now I may go to prison, too. Please help us as soon as you receive this.

Your very humble and affectionate daughter,
Lydia Wickham

Folding the letter, Algernon donned his brightest smile. "It seems she needs a bit of an advance on her yearly income for a particular ball gown she claims she cannot do without."

A cry for money was hardly a compliment to Lydia and so would be believed, leaving no reason for conjecture, but he dared not look at Elizabeth. His Lizzy was the one person he could not fool.

The moment Algernon had the privacy of his own room, he reread the letter. Lydia's handwriting was usually careless, and this letter was barely legible. She had to have been terrified when she wrote it. He had to protect her, and his first impulse was to send a bank note immediately.

After a moment, he realized, even if he knew the amount, it might not be wise to send it. Lydia had not returned the travel money he sent for her to attend her mother's funeral. Who knows where that money went. If he sent money now, Wickham might try to double it at a gaming table.

Without calling a servant, Algernon packed his valise, preparing to leave. He had to go to Lydia, settle her debt, and keep her out of prison.

There was a soft knock on the door. He opened it and turned away. Elizabeth entered and, without looking at her, he thrust Lydia's letter into her hand.

"Father, I can barely read...." She struggled a moment, then gasped. "This is terrible."

"Hill forwarded the letter at once, but I have already lost two days. I must leave for Norfolk first thing in the morning."

"Let me talk to Darcy. I am certain he will want to help and—"

Algernon held up his hand, silencing her. "He has already done enough for our Lydia."

Though Algernon always avoided being carried away by gratitude, he could not forget the event that put him forever in Darcy's debt. Before Darcy and Elizabeth were married, Lydia had consented to an elopement and run off with Wickham. Marriage, however, had not been his object. Unabashed, Lydia hid in London with him. Despite his dislike of the man, Darcy had hunted them down and bribed Wickham into marriage, saving Lydia from ruin and the Bennet family from disgrace. Algernon could not let Darcy save Lydia a second time.

Of course, there was no point in being too hasty.

Algernon thought it over. Darcy was rich and would not miss, how much? Fifty pounds? One hundred and fifty? He caught himself. "Elizabeth, this time the expense will rest where it belongs. Tell Darcy if you must, but I will not accept his help."

At dawn, Elizabeth had a carriage waiting, and after a quick breakfast, Algernon set off. When he changed to the post, he traveled through unfamiliar landscapes. He tried to pick out views for sketches but was unable to concentrate. He was lost in worry and could almost wish Mary was distracting him with her chatter. In his plot to leave her behind at Pemberley, he had intended to be called away on urgent business. No excuse he invented could have been as urgent as what actually called him away.

He spent the night on the road. When he arrived in Norfolk early the following day, all he had to do was find Lydia's lodgings, settle her bills, save the Wickhams from imprisonment, and persuade them both to stay out of trouble. He heaved a sigh.

Chapter 8

Algernon paid a hackney coach a shilling to take him to the Wickhams' address. The long ride took him through a crowded and shabby part of the town, and finally the coach stopped in front of a large, dilapidated house with a *Lodgings* sign hanging askew on the gate.

Algernon viewed the place with apprehension. Telling the coachman to wait, he went to the door, set his valise down on a ragged mat, and knocked. A woman answered and stared first at him, then at the valise.

"Tomorrow I will have better, but now my only room is on the top floor. A shilling a night or four shillings for five nights. I get my money before you get the room."

"My dear lady," Algernon said, smiling at one of the most hostile faces he had ever seen, "I am not here for a room. I am visiting my daughter, Mrs. Wickham."

The woman sneered. "Your daughter, is she? She is here, but she gets put out tomorrow. They can find those scoundrels a bed in prison."

After this warm greeting, Algernon dismissed the coach and went inside. The woman pointed him up the stairs. "Their room is down the hallway to the left."

"Lydia." Walking up the stairs, he called out her name and a door flung open.

Lydia rushed into his arms. "Papa! So glad. Help me, please. Only have until tomorrow." Her words were garbled. Her hair, pinned up on one side, had fallen loose on the other. The yellow dress she wore looked disheveled; dark rings encircled her eyes.

Algernon had to be firm. He had to be strict. Wickham was not blameless, but Lydia had to share responsibility for her situation. He put an arm around her—surely that was not too forgiving—and felt her whole body tremble with sobs. He patted her shoulder. "There, there," he said gruffly, determined to let her know tears did not soften him.

"Dearest Papa, I am so frightened. I have been hoping, praying, you would come."

Holding his hand, she tugged him into the room. The shabbiness matched the rest of the house. There was an unmade bed, an old table, a few chairs, a wooden chest, and little else.

"Where is your husband?" Algernon asked.

"At camp. I do not know when he will be back. Here, Papa, please sit down."

He eased into a rickety, wooden chair, uncertain whether it would hold his weight. She hovered at his side.

"Lydia, I will see the magistrate and arrange to pay your debt. How much do you owe?" he asked, bracing himself.

Lydia hung her head. "Twenty pounds."

Algernon was relieved. He had expected it to be a great deal more.

She did not look up. "We have to move."

"Your proprietress graciously informed me."

"She is Mrs. Pultney. She...does not like us."

"So I gathered. Do not fret. I am sure we can find you a decent place to live," he said, keeping his voice stern.

"Papa, you are so good. I would make you tea, but I dare not ask Mrs. Pultney for hot water."

Lydia asked about her sisters, especially Kitty, who had been her devoted partner in mischief, but Algernon was too preoccupied with the situation to recollect casual family news. Lydia, usually noisy and boisterous, was soon quiet, too. They waited in near silence until Wickham arrived. Algernon rose to greet him, trying for a scowl to equal the one that had greeted him at the front door.

"Mr. Bennet!"

Algernon declined to accept his extended hand. Instead of noticing, Wickham embraced him. "Sir, words cannot express the terrible grief we feel over the death of dear Mrs. Bennet."

"Poor Mama. I cannot believe I will never see her again." Lydia burst into tears. Wickham stopped embracing Algernon and comforted his wife.

Algernon cleared his throat. "We have important matters to discuss," he said, his frown in place.

"I am afraid so," Wickham said. "We have got ourselves into a bit of a mix-up."

"A bit of a mix-up," Algernon repeated. "Is that what you call a situation that might put my daughter in prison?"

"Sir, I spent the morning with Colonel Laurence and convinced him to give me another chance." Smiling, Wickham looked like a model of virtue. "He is getting me an advance on my stipend to pay our debt and find a place to live. If it comes through tomorrow, we will be all right."

Wickham hesitated. "If it does not come through, I will be forced to ask for your kind assistance."

"Papa will settle with the magistrate tomorrow. He will help us find a place to live."

Wickham expressed his gratitude with the sort of promises which had proved so untrustworthy in the past. Sitting down on the chest, he reached for his wife's hand. "I have something for you." He took a small box from his pocket.

Watching Lydia open it, Algernon wondered what a man in Wickham's situation could afford to buy.

"Dried cherries," she said, a woebegone smile lighting her tear-streaked face. "My favorite."

A box of cherries certainly did not set things right, but Wickham seemed remarkably proud of his gift. "Have you told your father our news?"

"Not yet."

"Then let me tell him. Sir, in the spring, we will welcome your grandson or granddaughter into the world."

Algernon knew it was a situation calling for a smile. He tried hard, but a smile was more challenging than a frown. It was not at all reassuring to think of these irresponsible people with a baby.

"I know in the past—in fact, our present situation—might make it seem we are not prepared to raise a child," Wickham said, sounding inappropriately cheerful.

"Might, indeed," said Algernon.

"I assure you, we will be good parents. Colonel Laurence has agreed to give me extra duty to increase my stipend and in the future, we will live within our means."

Although Wickham's talent for deception was well-honed, Algernon almost believed him. Almost.

Wickham continued. "My parents are dead. I never had another relative. This child will be very special to me."

When Wickham and Lydia were married, he had expressed delight in having sisters-in-law. Since he had been bribed to marry Lydia after living with her for a month, his words had sounded hollow. Now it seemed he might have been telling the truth. He was a rascal, but even a rascal might value family. At least, he had valued his wife's circumstance enough to bring her cherries when he had not known Algernon would be there to be impressed.

Algernon had to admit fatherhood had not enhanced his own character. Hopefully, it would improve Wickham's. If he gave up gambling and blaming others for his mistakes, he might come close to respectability. Lydia was not promising, but experience and motherhood might improve her. He gave up scowling and managed a response. "Good news indeed! All the more reason for us to get your affairs settled."

Though it would have cost only a shilling, he declined to sleep with Mrs. Pultney's roof over his head and spent the night in a nearby inn. In the morning, he joined the Wickhams at the magistrate's office. Waiting to be summoned, they sat on a long, plank bench and watched as several people were hauled off to prison. Lydia, so noisy and carefree in former days, huddled between husband and father.

Algernon stroked her hand. "It will be all right," he said as harshly as he could.

"Wickham!" The clerk called out the name.

Taking command, Algernon identified himself and said there had been a mistake in their records, and they were prepared to settle their debts. He paid the twenty pounds, glad he never left Longbourn without filling his money belt. After paying a fee to the magistrate, they were excused. Lydia rushed toward the door, seeming not to breathe until they left the building.

A light rain was falling, and Wickham was solicitous in holding an umbrella over Lydia. "I know a nice house for let," he said, turning toward Algernon. "Of course, I will not be able to afford it for several months. I doubt it will still be available." He put a bit of pathos into his voice.

Algernon had resigned himself to a debt of at least fifty pounds. Now he had a thirty-pound balance to assist them with lodgings and, trying to sound noncomittal, suggested they take a look at the house.

The rain was getting heavier. Walking as fast as they could, they headed to a house with a porch and small garden. The owner lived in a large house on the other side of the garden. He looked askance at Lydia and Wickham but was sufficiently impressed with Algernon to accept an initial payment on a twelve-month leasehold.

The house, though small, was a decided improvement over their former lodgings, and the existing furniture was sufficient to serve basic needs. Seeming more like her old self, Lydia dashed from room to room, calling out ideas for settling in and designating an alcove for the baby.

Algernon was pleased with an enormous bookcase which completely covered the sitting room wall. In any establishment, he would consider a place for books a necessity. Only a few, tattered volumes were on the shelves, likely left behind by a former tenant, but they were better than nothing. If confined to the house during winter, Lydia might finally develop the habit of reading.

The house put Wickham farther from his camp than formerly, but he said he did not mind and could walk in all but the worst weather.

When the rain stopped, they returned to Mrs. Pultney's for Wickham and Lydia to collect their belongings and for Algernon to settle their bill. Mrs. Pultney snatched her payment out of his hand.

Seeming disappointed, she said, "I suppose this means those two do not go to prison."

"I am afraid so," Algernon said. "Try to endure the disappointment."

Algernon thought the three of them made a charming picture as they walked in parade to the new house. Wickham led the way, stooping forward and carrying the chest on his back. Lydia followed, carrying a basket of clothes. Algernon brought up the rear, pushing a wheelbarrow piled high with the rest of their belongings.

He stayed another day to be sure Lydia and Wickham were settled. Her natural good spirits had returned, though she was not as boisterous as in former days, which could be viewed as desirable. Wickham was as glib and pleasing as ever. Despite better judgment telling him not to take his son-in-law too seriously, Algernon was impressed with his optimism and plans for the future.

Lydia's tears gushed when they said goodbye. Algernon felt moved and closer to her than he ever had. He returned her embrace, kissed her cheek, and abandoned all attempts to look severe.

On the journey home, he had time to think. Wickham's joy at the prospect of a family was disturbing. Although it was comforting to know his son-in-law took a responsible view of fatherhood, Algernon had to admit the birth of his own children had failed to reform him. As a parent, he had been indolent. He defended himself nobly, but even his best effort could not blame his behavior on Mrs. Bennet's unreasonableness and bad temper. The fault was his own.

If he had it to do over again....

But he did not. Realization had come too late. He could never be a good father.

Chapter 9

When the carriage turned down the hedgerow-lined lane, Algernon felt a surge of appreciation. Longbourn was a modest estate, the house was showing its age, but the fields and gardens blended one season into another with a beauty forever new.

Summer was his favorite season, at least from June until August. In September, his preference always shifted to the autumn until the first snowfall. Then he delighted in winter until the snow gave way to the coming of another vibrant spring. Now autumn was in charge. Trees were a spangle of bright yellow, rich gold and deep red leaves that drifted down to create the crackle underfoot that he loved on his morning walks.

He had wanted a son to inherit his beloved Longbourn, not to perpetuate himself, but to provide for his wife and daughters after his death. Now his wife was dead, his daughters situated. Family responsibilities were no longer a worry. His regret was that William Collins was an officious fool whom he could neither like nor respect. The man would view Longbourn in terms of pounds sterling. He would be aware the house needed paint and never notice the beauty of its setting.

Hill curtsied as he entered the house. "Sir, there have been several callers. Their cards are on your desk. The express letter from Miss Elizabeth—I mean, Mrs. Darcy—came the day before yesterday."

"Thank you, Hill."

Algernon did not inquire as to how Longbourn had fared during his absence. Had there been a catastrophe, he would have been told immediately. A problem short of catastrophe could wait.

Settling himself behind his desk, he read Elizabeth's letter. She had written to him at Longbourn, obviously convinced he would not return to Pemberley after he saw Lydia. Her first words told him he was a grandfather. The letter summoning her to the Bingleys had arrived shortly after he left, and Jane's confinement had gone well. Healthy and beautiful, Bennet Bingley had joined the world. Jane was recovering and very happy. Bingley had already assumed the role of doting father.

Elizabeth ended her letter with a carefully worded inquiry about Lydia. Algernon could imagine her almost holding her breath as she wrote, asking if he had arrived in time to assist her youngest sister.

Algernon immediately arranged paper and opened his inkbottle. *My Dear Jane.*

He wrote in his concise style, congratulating his eldest daughter and her husband and expressing joy at having a grandson.

After he folded and addressed Jane's letter, he wrote to Elizabeth. He told her Lydia's problem had been taken care of. His words were circumspect enough for her to show the letter if she wished to. He included the Wickhams' new address and did not share the news of their springtime expectation. He would leave the announcement to the Wickhams. He knew Elizabeth sent them money she saved from personal economies and had no doubt that when the new Wickham arrived, she would lavish gifts on her second nephew or first niece.

After the long carriage ride, Algernon needed exercise. He checked the rest of his mail, enjoyed a brisk walk of the grounds, and carefully noted that all his trees and shrubberies were exactly where he had left them. Returning to the house, he examined the calling cards left in his absence. Several were from neighbors who had visited regularly since Mrs. Bennet's death, trying to comfort his bereavement.

He stared at the names for a long moment, not indifferent to their concern for him.

He was surprised to see William Collins' card and doubted the man's motivation was so thoughtful. More likely, he had made the trip from Kent to check the paint on Longbourn house. He was a vulture circling his prey, but a self-respecting vulture waited until the prey was dead.

Setting the cards aside, Algernon told himself he had visited Elizabeth, provided for Mary, and rescued Lydia. More could not be expected of him. His daughters were gone; he was single again, and could do whatever he pleased. He admitted he had long been in the habit of doing whatever he pleased, but now there was nothing to distract him while he was doing it.

In the days that followed, Algernon found being alone quite comfortable, but he did not view himself as a recluse. He appreciated every dinner invitation and was not averse to accepting a few. Without his wife at his side to embarrass him with her loud and mindless chatter, he enjoyed being in company. He even considered inviting guests to Longbourn. He did not, of course, yet felt gracious knowing he had given it consideration.

Occasionally, he carried a gun under his arm during his morning tramps, an odd habit because he almost never shot at anything. Years earlier, he had brought down a pheasant and, looking at the bird's variegated and beautiful plumage, he had imagined it soaring in the sky instead of lifeless with staring eyes full of reproach. From then on, he shot only at mud hens. Pheasants and other beautiful birds had to fly to his neighbors' properties to get their chance to become a meal. He was not opposed to *eating* pheasant. On the table, with the beautiful feathers out of sight and the eyes lost with the head, he found the bird tasty.

Shortly before Christmas, the post brought two letters on the same day. Elizabeth's letter was chatty and mentioned that Darcy had assisted Andrew Pepper to obtain a commission in the navy. She said Mary would accompany them to the Bingleys where they would spend the holidays, and she urged him to join them. The letter from Jane contained her own sweet invitation, encouraging him to be with them for Bennet's first Christmas.

Algernon was rather sure young Master Bennet would not note his absence. Come spring, he would make his grandson's acquaintance. Now he much preferred to stay home. He waited a suitable number of days, then answered the letters, hoping the delay would support his claim of having given the matter serious consideration.

He received a letter from Mary by return post. It changed everything:

My dearest father, I will not leave you all alone on the first Christmas since my dear mother was swept up by the angels. Colonel Fitzwilliam is taking Miss Georgiana to spend the holidays with their aunt. They will very kindly route through Hertfordshire and deliver me to my parental abode. I promise to lighten your spirit as you endure the holidays without your beloved companion, and I shall keep the lonely walls soundly reverberating with songs of the blessed season.

Algernon cupped his hands over his ears just thinking about hearing the walls reverberate. Mary must stay where she was. This was one letter he had to answer immediately, but how could he tell her not to come? Longbourn was indeed her parental abode. He delayed writing one day and then another. If he did not take action, Mary would be on her way.

While pondering what to do, he reread Jane's letter. Then he reread the letter from Elizabeth. She had written something he had paid little attention to. Now it gave him a spark of hope. Mr. Pepper had received a commission in the Royal Navy, which meant his sister would probably be alone when he was assigned to a ship. She and Mary seemed to have forged a quick friendship and, with her brother gone, Miss Pepper might like to pay Mary a visit, a long visit.

What was her Christian name? Pondering, he decided it might be Dorinda. Well, he mused, if Miss Dorinda Pepper came to Longbourn, she would take up much, if not all, of Mary's time. He could still enjoy Longbourn and his privacy. If songs of the season set the walls reverberating, he could escape out-of-doors or take refuge in his library.

He wrote immediately, included an invitation to Miss Pepper, and sent the letter express.

Chapter 10

Algernon was going over his accounts when several neighbors came to report a death. Usually, the parson would be informed first, but that would not do in this case. The dead man was the parson. Algernon heard the news with regret and, acknowledging his responsibility as squire, set out for the parsonage.

Old Mr. Hendrick had enjoyed the affection of his parish, and it was overlooked when, in his later years, he occasionally confused the holy days. One Christmas Eve, he preached about the crucifixion and urged his parishioners to practice fasting and self-denial when they returned home. On a wet Easter morning, when they lowered their umbrellas, parishioners were surprised to see the baby Jesus asleep in a manger surrounded by a proper complement of wooden shepherds and angels. When it was time for a hymn, Parson Hendricks led a boisterous rendering of *O Come All Ye Faithful.* Algernon relished these little lapses. They provided his most reverent moments in church.

Letting his mind wander, he decided that in Mr. Hendrick's honor, instead of a proper burial service, perhaps a baptism, maybe a May Day celebration, would be seemly. He shook his head, forcing such thoughts out of mind. He looked properly grave when he offered brief and sincere condolences to the widow.

Despite swollen eyes and tear-stained cheeks, the lady's smile was warm. "Mr. Bennet, how good of you to come. Please sit down."

The seat of the chair she offered was frayed and patched with red wool. Algernon inspected the rest of the room. Tidy, cozy and shabby, very shabby— it could be described no other way. This was certainly not his first visit to the parsonage. How could he never have noticed the shabbiness before?

Mr. Hendrick had been parson of Longbourn church when Algernon inherited the estate. He had never considered replacing him, nor had he inquired about the annual income the parish provided, supposing—if he thought of it at all—that it was about two or three hundred pounds per annum, an ample sum. Now he wondered if the income had been half that amount.

He should have helped Hendrick by increasing his cowherd, granting him more pasture, or helping him increase his tithes. A rush of guilt followed anger. Why did he identify his responsibilities when it was too late to meet them?

At least he could assist the widow. "I want you to know the parsonage is your home for as long as it suits you. You need never leave."

"How kind you are."

Algernon did not feel kind and wanted to do more. "Is there anyone in particular you would like to conduct the service for your husband?"

"No, I do not think—" Mrs. Hendrick broke off, then said softly, "Perhaps there is someone. My dear husband was very fond of the young curate at Hamstone church." She shook her head. "But Hamstone is a long way off."

"Would you like him to come?"

"I am sure it is much too far." She hesitated again. "But if it would not be too much trouble." At Algernon's request, she told him the curate's name.

"Ian Marshall," Algernon said, repeating it. "Mrs. Hendrick, I shall go to Hamstone, and engage Mr. Marshall for your husband's service."

"Mr. Bennet, you are always so thoughtful."

Thoughtful indeed. After years of indifference, he would arrange for a curate of the parson's choice to conduct his burial service. If Algernon had not struggled against it, he would have felt ashamed.

He ordered his carriage and was soon on the way to Hamstone, nearly ten miles away. He had considered sending a servant with a letter, then decided it was his personal responsibility.

When he arrived at the parsonage of Hamstone church, he was shown into the sitting room. The parson, Mr. Worthington, was a man whose girth exceeded portly by an impressive margin, and he struggled to rise from his chair. "Mr. Bennet," he said, his cheeks puffing up in a smile, "it has been a long time since you and I last saw each other."

The man's size would make him memorable. Algernon was quite sure they had never met. "Mr. Worthington," he said, heartily shaking the offered hand, "what a pleasure to greet an old friend."

He accepted a sherry and quickly explained the reason for his visit.

Mr. Worthington shook his head. "Mr. Marshall attends to parish business, and he does not have transportation to travel to Longbourn. I am sorry I cannot oblige."

"Mr. Marshall can return to Longbourn with me. I will send him back in my carriage," Algernon said, suspecting Worthington did not want his curate to leave because then *he* would have to attend to parish business.

"By the way," he added, beaming as if struck by a happy thought. "Do you like apricot brandy? I have some that is quite superior. I preserve it carefully, and it would be my pleasure to have him bring you back a bottle."

Mr. Worthington's puffy cheeks got puffier. He immediately summoned a servant and sent him to find Mr. Marshall. Algernon was treated to vapid chatter until the young man arrived, breathless from running.

"This is Mr. Bennet," Mr. Worthington said. "You must go with him and conduct the burial for Mr. Hendrick."

Marshall's smile of greeting faded. "For Mr. Hendrick? When did he die?"

"Early this morning," Algernon told him.

"I am sorry," Marshall said, his expression matching his words. "He and I once had a good, long chat. He was very kind and encouraged me. I shall never forget him."

Mr. Worthington was not going to be done out of good brandy and had ordered his curate to go. Algernon preferred to make a request. "Mrs. Hendrick told me her husband thought very well of you. We would both be grateful if you would be kind enough to return to Longbourn with me for his burial."

"I am honored," Marshall said.

"I look forward to tasting that rare brandy," Mr. Worthington said when Mr. Marshall left to get ready.

"And you shall," Algernon said, trying to remember what kind of brandy he had promised. *Apricot*, that was it. He had to send to the village to buy a bottle.

On the return trip to Longbourn, they were slowed by the first snowfall of the season. Bored, Algernon decided to test Mr. Marshall's amusement value. He began with casual conversation, asking where he was from and how long he had been in orders.

"I am from Warwickshire," Marshall said. "I was ordained last spring." He spoke pleasantly and did not expand his answers. Algernon tried again.

"You must have felt a strong calling to enter the church." Algernon leaned back, sure this opportunity would allow Mr. Marshall to expound on how the light had shone and the angels beckoned.

"No," Ian Marshall said. "I have a respect for the church and try to do a good job. However, I took orders because I needed an income. My only other option was to continue tutoring." His voice dropped. "I think I made the better choice."

His tutoring post must have been dismal if employment with Mr. Worthington was preferable. Algernon studied him. He was tall and appeared thin, though surely in the same room with Mr. Worthington almost anyone would appear thin.

"I am twenty-four," Mr. Marshall said. "The position with Mr. Worthington was the only one offered me. I was happy to accept it."

The man was so forthright, Algernon lost the urge to expose his follies and let conversation slow until the carriage turned up the lane to Longbourn.

After breakfast the next morning, Mr. Marshall left to go to the parsonage. "I want to talk to Mrs. Hendrick and find out if there is a particular reading she would like at the service," he said.

The following day, Mr. Hendrick was laid to rest in the graveyard of the church he had served. The sermon sending him on his way was not laden with limitless praise but made clear the life ended had been well lived. Algernon was impressed with Marshall's direct style and decided to invite him to stay two days longer and conduct the Sunday service. Mr. Worthington could conduct his own service. Perhaps, in compensation, he should be gifted with two bottles of that rare brandy.

Chapter 11

When Algernon asked him to remain until Sunday, Ian Marshall hesitated. "Mr. Worthington would not approve."

They were alone at dinner. Watching the curate heap his plate with potatoes and pork, Algernon wondered about meals at Hamstone parsonage. That Mr. Worthington ate well was a certainty, and it was possible his young assistant took meals in the kitchen, feasting on whatever tidbits were not consumed in the dining room.

Algernon signaled the butler to refill Marshall's soup bowl. "I will post a letter to Mr. Worthington and promise him our special cheese to go with our special brandy. I am sure he will think it a fair trade for allowing us your services."

When Marshall put down his fork, he said, "Sir. I promise to work hard on my sermon."

Algernon wanted to caution him not to work too hard, in case effort and length were commensurate.

On Sunday, when Ian Marshall took his place at the pulpit, Algernon had little hope of being entertained. Today's sermon could not be expected to have the value of Hendrick's confusion of holidays, and there was something rational about the young man that did not loan itself to the ridiculous.

Marshall began to speak, then cleared his throat and coughed. Instead of continuing his sermon, he said, "You good people do not want to listen to me cough. Give me a moment, and I will pretend I am not nervous." His smile made him look younger than his twenty-four years.

He had not seemed nervous officiating at Mr. Hendrick's funeral. Algernon wondered why he was uneasy now, and understood the moment Marshall cast a furtive glance in his direction. It was the young man's first time in Longbourn pulpit. He did not want it to be his last. Mr. Hendrick's death left the church without a parson, and he was making it known he was available.

Algernon crossed his arms and relaxed as much as the narrow pew would allow. He assured himself he was not a man who made snap decisions, his decision to propose marriage the exception. He would add Mr. Marshall's name to the list, but finding the right parson would take time and effort.

Even before Mr. Hendrick was consigned to the ground, the community had risen to the occasion with eager recommendations of worthy kindred to take his place. In making a selection, Algernon had to learn as much as he could about several of the more promising candidates. He had an obligation to his tenants to make a thoughtful and intelligent choice.

When Mr. Marshall quieted his nerves, he gave a pleasant sermon that, brilliantly, did not last too long. Following his usual custom, Algernon strode out of church before the last strains of the benediction faded.

"Mr. Bennet! Mr. Bennet!"

He turned back as several people called to him: "Is this young man going to be our new parson?"

"Such a nice man."

"I hope he is going to stay with us."

"I like him!"

"Is he married?"

"*That* is what *I* was going to ask." Mrs. Long sounded annoyed. Perhaps the first woman to ask was entitled to first try at snagging a single man for a daughter.

Algernon returned home, pleased that Marshall had been so well-received, and waited until the young man had finished dinner before ordering the carriage. In addition to the brandy, Algernon had

Hill pack a large cheese and a mince pie for Mr. Worthington. Surely, the unexpected pie and cheese would keep him from being too annoyed because of his curate's extended absence.

Before Mr. Marshall left, Algernon paid him a crown.

"Thank you, Sir," he said. "This is almost what I am paid each month."

Algernon was startled at such a paltry income but tactfully did not mention it. He poured them both a sherry. "Our parishioners seemed pleased with you."

"I appreciated my stay here."

"Mr. Marshall, what is your commitment to Mr. Worthington?"

"Sir, I have been with him for eleven months, and we have no agreement."

"I daresay you will be with him a long time," Algernon said, not wanting to foster hopes.

Marshall's voice went flat. "I am fortunate to have the position."

"If a crown is nearly a month's salary, he pays you pitifully," Algernon said, forgetting to be tactful.

"Mr. Worthington said he would increase my stipend after I was with him six months."

"I take it the worthy Mr. Worthington has not kept his word."

"It was never mentioned again," Marshall said quickly. "I am sure Mr. Worthington has forgotten."

When the butler announced that the carriage was ready, Marshall rose from his chair and seemed unsure of whether to extend his hand. Algernon quickly offered his.

Algernon threw his great coat on his shoulders, and together they went outside. On route to the carriage, the young man stopped and looked toward a stand of snow-glazed trees. "Longbourn is a wonderful place and has very beautiful grounds," he said. "I enjoyed my walks here very much."

The coachman opened the door. Marshall put his foot on the step.

"Mr. Marshall, will you accept the position of parson of Longbourn church?"

Ian Marshall looked surprised, although not as surprised as Algernon felt hearing the words escape his mouth.

This time, Marshall did not hesitate and grasped Algernon's hand. "Mr. Bennet, thank you. I promise to work hard. I will do a good job."

Algernon retrieved the hand Marshall jerked up and down. "Indeed, Sir," he said, uncomfortable at being the dispenser of so much joy. "But before you accept, I must tell you, I cannot offer you the parsonage. I have promised it to Mrs. Hendrick for life."

"I am sure I can find a family in the village to board with."

"Or you could live at Longbourn." Algernon blinked hard. Had that been his voice? Recovering his senses, he added a quick, "Of course, you would undoubtedly be happier boarding with a family."

"Staying at Longbourn would be better than anything I could hope for."

Algernon could not imagine what had possessed him to offer Marshall both the church and a bed under his own roof. Perhaps he had simply felt sorry for someone unfortunate enough to be an underling to Mr. Worthington, and perhaps—he could not totally dismiss the thought—he liked the man.

The basket for Mr. Worthington was placed in the carriage, and Marshall still stood, one foot on the step. "I am helping several people in Hamstone. I should finish what I started, and Mr. Worthington will want time to replace me. Then I will come as soon as you want me."

"Anytime will do," Algernon said. He turned and fled into the house.

Chapter 12

S tudying the view from his window, Algernon sketched his beloved trees. An ink drawing could not do justice to the sunlight on the snow-laden boughs, but he caught the play of shadows rather well.

His thoughts went to Ian Marshall, and he decided offering him Longbourn pulpit had been brilliant. It saved him the bother of evaluating candidates, and Marshall was surely as good as any and better than most.

There was nothing disagreeable about the man and, after his cheerful experience with Worthington, he would work hard to secure a permanent post. As for his boarding at Longbourn, the house had been a comfortable home for five daughters; there had to be room for one clergyman. He could take his meals in the kitchen or his room, except when invited to the dining parlor.

The sketch was almost finished and, studying it, he decided the perspective was wrong. The trees in the background were too large. Smaller, they would have portrayed the idea of distance better.

Hill knocked on the door. "Sir, the post is here."

Accepting two letters, he read Elizabeth's first and then Mary's:

My Dear Father, I thank you for telling me I could invite Dorinda to Longbourn. We have become good friends and both look forward to her long visit. As you see, she is Dorinda to me now, not Miss Pepper. We will arrive....

Closing one eye, Algernon squinted, but the next word was still legible. *Friday.* They would be here the day after tomorrow.

He read the rest of her letter, surprised it was forthright, without a quotation or line of poetry. She must have been rushed to write so sensibly.

The next morning, he told the servants guests would be arriving on the morrow. "Miss Mary's friend will remain for some time," he said to Hill. "Miss Darcy and Colonel Fitzwilliam will probably stay the night. Do whatever you do to assure an especially fine dinner." He waved her away when she asked what dishes he would like served. What constituted a fine dinner was not his concern.

He emptied a large pouch of coins onto his desk and, reviewing a list of Longbourn servants, began apportioning Christmas monies. Other people's servants might occasionally venture into dishonesty, and he was grateful his were a trustworthy lot. Christmas was the time he showed his appreciation.

Algernon suspected life was easier for Hill since Mrs. Bennet's death. She no longer had to sooth excitable nerves or meet unreasonable demands and, without a mistress, she was in full charge of the household and very efficient. He added an extra crown to her pile.

A carriage was approaching, and the weather was too nasty for casual callers. He resigned himself to Mary's arrival a day sooner than expected, but the voice he heard was not Mary's. "Lady Lucas," he said, going to the entry to greet her. He wanted to say it was a pleasant surprise, but doubted the occasion required his redesigning truth.

Sir William and Mr. Collins followed her. A small boy was bundled in Mr. Collins' arms.

"My poor Mr. Bennet," Lady Lucas said, "we worry about you and had to call."

"Noble sir," Mr. Collins said, slightly inclining his head.

Feeling neither poor nor noble, he accompanied his guests into the drawing room.

"We arrived at Lucas Lodge yesterday. My dear wife wanted to pay this visit with us, but she is still weary from traveling. She again has a condition."

Mr. Collins sat down, holding the result of her first condition on his lap.

"Mr. Collins, put little William down so poor Mr. Bennet can see how splendidly he walks." Lady Lucas extended her arms toward the child.

Mr. Collins set the boy on his feet. To the delight of his relations, he managed to take tottering steps toward his grandmother.

"Upon my word," Algernon said in amazement. "A biped."

"A bi- what?" Sir William asked.

"A biped," Mr. Collins repeated grandly. "It means something that walks on two feet."

"I am certain someday he will walk on two feet into St. James," Sir William said.

"He can talk, too," the grandmother added. "Just yesterday, he said two words. We were not sure what he meant, but they were very clear."

Algernon restrained his laughter. People could be absurd in praise of their progeny.

It was Mr. Collins' turn: "He is large for his age. Mother Lucas, did dear Charlotte tell you he has already outgrown his second set of clothes?"

"Elizabeth says Bennet Bingley is the strongest baby the midwife has ever seen." It was possible she had actually written that the midwife thought he was a strong, healthy baby. He could not be expected to get a quote exactly right.

"Really?" Lady Lucas said, her eyebrows sliding upward. "Little William is amazingly strong."

"I am told Bennet is quite a handsome child." Algernon was stating facts, not boasting about his descendant. Kindly, he refrained from adding any Bingley child would be better looking than this child. The poor thing already showed an unpleasant resemblance to his father.

Picking up his son, Mr. Collins went to a window and pulled the drape wide to expose the view. "Look, William. Is this not a fine place?" he said, the pride in his voice not disguised.

"Do be sure to tell him he stands in direct line to inherit Longbourn," Algernon said. "I am sure the knowledge will be exciting to a child his age."

"It seems to me," Mr. Collins mused, "that if you felled those trees to the west of the house, you could add considerably to the pasture. Indeed, the lumber itself would be very valuable." Suddenly, he gasped. "But of course there is no need—no reason at all—for you to bother felling the trees. I certainly would not do it if I were you."

Algernon realized his beautiful trees would fall to valuable lumber whenever Collins took possession of the estate. Since that event was predicated on his death, he would not see it happen. Still, the knowledge was painful. He had to respond. "I would never have thought of it," he said. "You are right and I thank you. In the spring, I will have all the trees felled. I daresay their sale will add nicely to my purse."

Mr. Collins had been robbed by his own words and looked gratifyingly stricken.

When the three doting adults took their biped home, Algernon hurried to his library, arranged a fresh sheet of paper, and began to draw. He had to get the trees right before Mr. Collins felled them.

Chapter 13

Howling winds rattled the wood shutters. By midday, swirling drifts of snow banked high against the house. It was not a day to be on the road. Algernon could not keep Mary and her traveling companions out of mind.

He knew Mrs. Bennet would have been fretting and imagining all manner of evils: *Their horses will slip and fall. The carriage will overturn when they are alone on the road.*

Had she been charging through the house and describing one disaster after another, he would have tried to convince her not to worry and been amused by her terrors. Without her to console and laugh at, he was plagued by anxieties of his own: Perhaps the horses *would* slip. The carriage *might* overturn.

At dinnertime, they still had not arrived. The fine meal Algernon had ordered would, at best, be served as a late supper. He declined his own dinner and paced from one room to another, occasionally stopping at a window to stare down the lane.

Night had long claimed the last of pale winter light when he heard the carriage. He swung the door open before the butler reached it and shouted into the wind. "Welcome, and hurry inside!"

Colonel Fitzwilliam and the coachman assisted Miss Darcy, Miss Pepper, and Mary down from the carriage and rushed them into the house. Greetings were brief. Conversation could wait for warmer times. After all wraps and boots were removed, they gathered around the fire in the drawing room where Algernon had tea and brandy served.

Miss Pepper stood with the other travelers, all hands extended toward the blaze. "Mr. Bennet," she said, turning to him and curtsying, "I appreciate your invitation to visit Longbourn."

"I hope your stay with us will be pleasant," he said, realizing he would not have known her had he encountered her unawares.

"Papa, we could not keep the coach heater lit, and the robes were not enough to keep us warm."

Inside the carriage it was cold. Algernon knew riding outside had to be miserable. He summoned the butler. "Take the coachmen and footman to the kitchen. See that they get a good drink to warm them and something to eat. They can bed down in the back room."

He turned to the colonel. "Sir, I am grateful to you for traveling so far out of your way to bring my daughter home. You and Miss Darcy must remain at Longbourn until the weather improves."

"He brought Miss Pepper, too," Mary said.

"Indeed. I thank him for that, also."

When hands were warmed and the stamping of feet was over, Algernon and his guests removed to the dining room. Anxious to reach Longbourn while travel was still possible, they had stopped only to change horses and had not eaten. Hill's table was so much enjoyed, Algernon could almost remember telling her what to serve.

After the guests had been shown their rooms, the entire party gathered downstairs. Algernon was pouring port for himself and the colonel when Hill wanted his attention.

"Sir, there is someone come to the door for you. He is frozen through and can barely speak."

"Did you recognize the carriage?"

"I saw no carriage. He comes on foot."

"Surely not on a night like this," Algernon said. Rather than have the caller shown into the drawing room, he went to the door.

"Mr. Bennet, I...am so sorry...to bother...." His teeth chattered so much, it was hard for him to speak. A thin scarf draped around his head, hiding his face. It took a moment, then recognition came.

"Marshall! How did you get here?"

"Walked. Got a ride for a distance in a farmer's dogcart. Had to come now. Mr. Worthington...so angry...."

"Angry because you are leaving him?"

Marshall removed the scarf and steadied himself. "Yes, Sir."

"Let us warm you up." Putting his hand on Marshall's shoulder, he led him toward the fire.

The ladies and Colonel Fitzwilliam stared at the half-frozen man who, despite his shabbiness, still maintained the air and manner of a gentleman when he acknowledged the ladies with a bow. All talking gave way to curiosity, and Algernon enjoyed the scene too much to end it with a quick explanation.

The room remained silent except for the snaps of the fire until Algernon said, "May I introduce Mr. Ian Marshall, the new parson of Longbourn church."

The ladies curtseyed to him; the colonel extended his hand. "Marshall," he said, testing the name. "There is a Captain Marshall in my regiment. Could he be a relative?"

Marshall shook his head. "My only relative is a brother, Alexander Marshall. He is the squire of Oakleigh in Warwickshire."

Algernon was surprised. Although the young man evidenced education and breeding, his obvious poverty, hardly suggested a close relationship with the landed gentry.

Miss Pepper whispered something to Mary, who then poured a brandy. "Sir," she said, handing it to Mr. Marshall.

"Oakleigh in Warwickshire," Algernon said, trying to restore conversation. "I am not familiar with it."

"I think I am," Colonel Fitzwilliam said. "It is a large estate, is it not?"

"Yes, Sir. People travel long distances to view the grounds. I spent much of my boyhood playing in the great woods."

The colonel looked surprised. "Then Oakleigh is your home."

"It was until my father died." As if answering their unvoiced question, he continued: "Alexander is my half-brother and many years older. He was married and living in London when I was born. I have never had the opportunity to know him well."

"I suppose he has many children," Algernon said, thinking only an abundance of offspring could keep the squire of a large estate from providing for a younger brother, half or whole.

"I am afraid not," Marshall said. "A year ago, he lost his only child and wife to the typhoid."

Clasping her hands together, Miss Darcy stared at the newcomer. "Oh, Sir, I am so very sorry. My own brother's wife is very dear to me. I can imagine how wretched you must feel."

Ian Marshall smiled. "Miss Darcy, you are very kind."

"I should not have asked about children. You had told us he was your only relative." Algernon's attempt at reviving conversation had ended with two deaths from the typhoid. He felt obliged to come up with something less gloomy. "Does that make you heir to the estate?"

"I am heir unless my brother remarries and has other children."

"If you and the squire are not attached, I daresay you do not drink to his long life." Perhaps it was not a proper remark, but his Lizzy would have been amused. His present companions looked stunned.

"I am sure what dear Mr. Bennet means," Miss Pepper said, "is that it is very regrettable you and your brother are not better acquainted."

It was audacious of Miss Pepper to interpret him. However, his guests looked relieved, and he felt obliged to say, "Of course, that is what I meant."

When the travelers retired, Algernon directed the maid to ready a room for yet another guest, and Mr. Marshall was shown upstairs. Alone, Algernon poured himself a brandy. Last night, Longbourn had been his exclusive domain. Tonight, he shared it

with four guests and a daughter. The colonel and
Miss Darcy were pleasant and would remain a day
or two at most. He was certainly accustomed to
Mary, and Mr. Marshall would not be a problem.
But there was something about Miss Pepper.

A tall woman, she carried herself unusually
erect, and her expression suggested she was often
privately amused. He had invited her to relieve
himself of Mary. Now he wondered if she might
become another pair of tight shoes. Tossing his
head back, he drained his glass.

Chapter 14

T he chestnut tree on the north lawn still churned hard against the wind. Yesterday's wet snow had frozen and gilded the landscape with slick, glistening ice. Algernon had to forego his morning tramp, and he waited in the breakfast parlor for his guests.

Voices announced the approach of Mary and Miss Pepper. They were soon followed by the colonel and, a few minutes later, by Miss Darcy. Noting Ian Marshall's absence, Algernon sent the butler to summon him, a particular invitation in case he did not feel entitled to join the other guests.

Mr. Marshall appeared and, after he got his breakfast at the sideboard, Algernon gestured him to the table. He seated himself next to Miss Darcy.

"Mr. Marshall," she said, "I do hope you are well after suffering such a chill last night."

Ian seemed preoccupied with his food but, lowering his fork, he smiled at her. "I am warm and well this morning. You are kind to be concerned."

"Mr. Bennet told us you will be staying at Longbourn. When I was here in the summer, my dear sister Elizabeth and I walked to Meryton. I think it is wonderful to be able to walk to town instead of going in a carriage. And this house is so pleasant."

"Yes, it is," Miss Pepper said. "One feels at home here very quickly."

"The grounds have much to offer," Marshall said between bites. "I enjoyed my walks here very much."

Miss Darcy nodded. "I am sure in summer the view from the bedroom window is delightful." Continuing, she mentioned how much she admired the painting of a flower garden she had noticed in the upstairs hall.

Thinking about the magnificent grounds and treasured artworks at Pemberley, Algernon was skeptical of Georgiana's great praise of Longbourn. Raising his eyebrows, he was about to say perhaps her brother would like to trade estates. He could not do it. The gentle girl spoke from her heart, and that she spoke so much was surprising. He had never before seen her eager to engage in conversation.

Colonel Fitzwilliam peered out the window. "It is starting to snow again. With the wind whipping it up, the coachman could not see as far as the horses. Mr. Bennet, I am afraid we must continue to impose on your hospitality."

"Impose on me! I am delighted to have you. You must not think of leaving until the weather improves."

Mary joined the colonel at the window. "It is often noted that weather plays an important role in human endeavors. Indeed, the success or failure of our farmers can often be predicted by seasonal temperatures and—" Stopping in mid-sentence, Mary clasped her hand over her mouth and looked quickly at Miss Pepper whose nod acknowledged communication.

Algernon wondered whether Miss Pepper had convinced Mary she need not sound erudite every time she said good morning. If so, the woman had some merit, but something about her manner made it hard to believe anyone could find her pleasing.

"Georgiana!" The colonel called his cousin a second time. She was talking to Mr. Marshall and had not responded before. Now he said, "My dear Georgiana, we must accept Mr. Bennet's gracious invitation and remain here until the snow lets up."

After breakfast, Algernon had a pleasant chat with the colonel, who agreed with him on a number of issues, thus demonstrating his intelligence. When he went to the library, he was startled to find Miss

Pepper standing by his desk, staring at something. "Well, well," he said.

Miss Pepper did not look up. "Sir, I hope I am not intruding. Miss Mary told me you would not mind if I selected a book from your collection, and this sketch caught my attention."

Algernon reached to snatch it but was too late. Miss Pepper picked it up and stepped to the window, comparing it to the scene it portrayed. "The trees are accurately drawn, especially the chestnut on the left. It is fine work, but I do not think the perspective is quite right."

Algernon stiffened. "You think the perspective is all wrong?"

"No, most is excellent, but the background trees could be smaller. Perhaps you made them larger to enhance the fine detail." She smiled. "I would very much like to see more of your drawings."

"Would you indeed," he said, not trying to mask his irritation. It had been careless of him to leave the sketch on his desk and audacious of this upstart woman, first to invade his privacy, then to criticize. Algernon relished his talent for wit and sarcasm, but his wife had been swept up for more than six months. Wit and sarcasm were out of practice. He could think of nothing piercing to say.

Miss Pepper returned the sketch to his desk, took a volume off the bookshelf, and held it out for his inspection. "Scott," she said. "You like him, too. He is my favorite, and I have not read this one. May I take it?"

He told her to take whatever she pleased, using a tone he hoped would tell her to leave and not come back. When she closed the door behind her, he studied the sketch. The perspective might not be quite right, although she had not allowed for the current snowfall, which made some of the trees look smaller. She had been accurate about the fine detail.

He wanted to go to his bedroom and, to avoid encountering his guests, used the back stairway by the kitchen. Approaching it, he heard laughter and expected to come upon servants. Instead, he found Miss Darcy and Mr. Marshall sitting on the stairs, engaged in a lively conversation. It was several minutes before they noticed him.

Mr. Marshall jumped to his feet, and they both talked at once. "Sir, I apologize. Miss Darcy expressed interest in seeing more of the house and I—"

"It is my fault. I love the house where dear sister Elizabeth grew up and—"

Algernon held up his hand, silencing them. "No apologies, please. You are perfectly welcome to tour the house. I must say, however, that the backstairs and the pantry are our less scenic areas."

He guessed their tour of the house had ended when conversation took precedence, and they found the stairs handy. They had been seated several stairs apart and, stepping past them, he made his way, leaving them alone. Apparently, they did not end their conversation, because at dinner they sat close to each other and talked in voices too soft to be heard by anyone else.

The next morning brought a break in the bad weather, and Colonel Fitzwilliam was in a rush to be gone. When Hill told Algernon they were ready to leave, he went to make his goodbyes.

Miss Darcy seemed more animated than he had ever seen her. "Mr. Bennet, I am so glad to have visited Longbourn again. I must tell my dear sister Elizabeth how much I like it."

"Miss Darcy, you must come to us again and stay longer. Mary and I would both be delighted to have you."

"Oh, I should very much like to come again."

Mary added a many-worded echo of Algernon's invitation, and Algernon sent the butler to warm Miss Darcy's heavy lap robe at the fire. While they waited, Colonel Fitzwilliam paid his courtesies. Algernon encouraged them by saying it was too cold for them to expect more snow. Although they might very well freeze on the journey, they need not fear being caught in a drift.

Algernon was surprised to see Mr. Marshall waiting at the carriage. As he handed Miss Darcy in, she paused. The two appeared to snatch a brief conversation until Colonel Fitzwilliam touched her, urging her up the step. She was waving when the driver cracked the whip to the horses. Mr. Marshall returned her wave and walked behind the carriage until it turned up the lane.

Chapter 15

Christmas usually afforded Algernon more pleasure than he admitted, yet he had no happy expectations for this holiday. He regretted his wife's death and never more than when Mary repeated her promise to provide music to commemorate the season.

"I will do my best to cheer us with songs of the glad tidings," she said, taking her place at the table.

Less than thrilled, Algernon quickly reminded her she had an obligation to Miss Pepper. "Your guest must not be left unattended and, splendid as it is, your music might pain us by bringing to mind happier times."

"Happier times!" she responded, unnecessarily cheerful. "Indeed, music will help chase away our heartfelt gloom. It is our duty to celebrate the holiday nobly in memory of my dear mother."

When breakfast was over, Mary anchored herself at the pianoforte. All too quickly, Algernon noted that what she lacked in talent, she still made up for in diligence. Hymns and cheery Christmas music sounded through the house all day and on the days that followed. Occasionally, Miss Pepper joined in a duet, but *Ivanhoe* took most of her time. The weather was still too severe to allow Algernon to escape out-of-doors, and the library was his only refuge. He had just finished his tea when there was a tap on the door.

"Come in, Sarah," he said.

"Mr. Bennet, I am not Sarah."

"Ah, Miss Pepper," he said crisply. "I suppose you have come for another book."

"Not another book. Sir, I am curious about the gift baskets for your tenants. I understand your steward will deliver them tomorrow."

"True. Mr. Stanley has done it for years."

"Perhaps this year, you will allow Miss Mary and me to deliver the baskets."

Algernon shook his head. "Mr. Stanley usually spends time at each house. He is gone most of the day and—" He stopped.

Mr. Stanley was gone most of the day.

"Miss Pepper, what an excellent idea."

"With your permission, I will tell Miss Mary. I think she will be pleased." Turning to leave, Miss

Pepper paused. "I do hope you will not mind being deprived of the delightful Christmas music while we are away."

"I will manage," he said solemnly.

She closed the door, and Algernon leaned back in his chair. It was quite amusing of Miss Pepper to think he would miss Mary's musical efforts. The foolish woman had no idea how pleased he would be to have a quiet day.

He received a number of invitations to holiday celebrations. Citing the black ribbons on his arm, he declined them all, but Sir William and Lady Lucas did not accept his regrets. They came early on the day before Christmas to argue their point, and they confronted Algernon, the ladies and Mr. Marshall in the breakfast parlor:

"My friend," Sir William said, "it would be no disrespect to your dear wife for you to come to such old friends tonight."

"Indeed, she would want all of you to come," his wife said, giving Mr. Marshall a warm smile.

Mary and Miss Pepper had delivered the baskets the previous day and sending them to the party would again deprive Algernon of Mary's delightful music. He was planning to decline for himself, yet accept for Mary when Miss Pepper said, "Mr. Bennet, if you do not want to attend, Miss Mary can represent the family."

Mary shook her head. "I do not want to leave dear Papa alone on Christmas Eve."

Not hearing Mary, Miss Pepper said, "Lady Lucas, will you need Miss Mary to play the piano?"

"Indeed. We must have music for dancing," Sir William said, answering for his wife.

Mary looked hesitant. "Perhaps, if you need me, but I should not—"

Algernon jumped in. "Of course, you must go if they need excellent music."

There was nothing more to discuss. Mary, Miss Pepper and Mr. Marshall would attend the party at Lucas Lodge. For the second time, Miss Pepper had unwittingly done him a service.

On Christmas Eve, Algernon was alone, but not lonely. A letter had arrived from Elizabeth, and he had the pleasure of reading it in solitude. It had been sent express, as were all her letters to him, allowing him to enjoy being one of the few extravagances of the newly rich Mrs. Darcy. She wrote they were still with the Bingleys, and much of her letter contained anecdotes about Bingley's delight at being a father.

He bought little Bennet a pony for Christmas. The baby cannot sit up yet. It was hard for us to conceal our amusement.

We received a letter from Georgiana and the following day, I received a letter addressed to me personally. She praised Longbourn, and she asked about your new parson, Mr. Ian Marshall. I am certain her interest in the young man was her reason for writing. She must have been impressed with him—surprising considering the briefness of their acquaintance.

Algernon was amazed that Georgiana had been bold enough to ask Elizabeth about Ian Marshall, but not surprised at her interest. Although a person without his perception might have missed it, he knew the two had caught each other's attention.

They met when Miss Darcy saw him being led half-frozen to the fire. He was the son of a squire, yet it was obvious the present squire, his own half-brother, did not acknowledge him. Certainly, he had an air of mystery and romance.

Algernon had never appraised Ian's looks before and now decided a young woman might think him handsome. Curly hair, more nearly black than dark brown, contrasted with his fair complexion and clear blue eyes. He lacked the awkwardness of many tall, thin men, and he had a boyish smile. Georgiana Darcy would rarely be called pretty, but Algernon's own regrettable matrimonial experience convinced him a good nature was more desirable in a wife than a lovely face.

If Ian Marshall did return Miss Darcy's interest, he had a competitor. Observing the colonel's attentions to her at Longbourn, Algernon was now convinced that his suspicions at Pemberley had been right. Fitzwilliam hoped to change Georgiana's status from cousin and ward to wife.

The colonel had much to recommend him, but if Algernon dabbled in matchmaking, his choice for her would be Ian Marshall. It would not be choosing her into poverty. In addition to her own inheritance, Ian was heir presumptive to a great estate, and men his brother's age did not father sons.

Algernon had disdained his wife's gossip about matches and possible matches. Relieved of matrimonial ties of his own, it surprised him to realize how entertaining it was to ponder couplings in the making.

Chapter 16

When everyone was in place, Algernon rose from his pew. He had never before made an announcement in church and immediately had unwavering attention: "On this fine morning, I take pleasure in introducing our new parson, Mr. Ian Marshall. Mr. Hendrick's admiration recommended him. He is our late parson's last service to us, and he will serve us well."

Resuming his seat, Algernon looked around at people nodding approval. Mrs. Hendrick beamed, the tears she dabbed at not dimming her smile.

Ian Marshall stepped into his new pulpit, said how grateful he was for the assignment, and promised to strive hard to live up to Mr. Hendrick's esteem. He made an excellent beginning by giving an encouraging holiday sermon and keeping it brief.

Algernon rarely opened his hymnal and never sang but, feeling proud of Ian and pleased with himself, he bellowed out the last hymn in a voice that had not lost volume through disuse.

After exchanging a litany of Merry Christmases, he extricated himself from the crowd and headed home, walking behind Mary and Miss Pepper.

As if in compliment to Christmas, the winter sun was unusually bright. Ice-glazed trees sparkled, and the cold air carried the tang of fresh snow. In the field, pristine drifts glittered as if scattered with jewels. Algernon wished he could capture the scene on his sketchpad.

Suddenly, Miss Pepper slipped on a patch of ice and fell backward, beating the air with her arms. Jerking to her aid, Algernon caught her hand and put his free arm around her waist to steady her.

"Thank you," she gasped, clutching his hand.

"Wait!" Lady Lucas and her husband hurried toward them. "Mr. Bennet, I think...I do think...." Lady Lucas suddenly went mute, affording Algernon the pleasure of not hearing her thought.

"Lady Lucas," Miss Pepper said, recovering, "I daresay you want to tell Mr. Bennet you are pleased with his choice of Mr. Marshall as our new parson."

"*Our* new parson," Lady Lucas repeated.

"He is quite the sort of person one meets at court," Sir William said.

"With dear Mrs. Bennet gone, he must be a burden at Longbourn," Lady Lucas said, recapturing her memory. "Do let him know he is welcome to reside with us." As she spoke, her breath formed white puffs in the cold air.

Algernon was quick to understand the invitation. Several unmarried daughters still adorned the Lucas home. If they secured Mr. Marshall under their roof before an undeserving young woman snared him, it would enhance their chance of marrying off a second daughter to a clergyman. Amused, he said, "Lady Lucas, Mr. Marshall is no trouble."

"But, Mr. Bennet, it would be better if—"

"A beautiful Christmas morning," Miss Pepper said, interrupting, "but too cold for us to linger."

Algernon withdrew his hand from her waist and offered his arm. "Indeed, my dear, much too cold." Mary took his other arm, and they walked home amid a fresh volley of Christmas greetings.

Algernon summoned the servants and distributed their gifts. He was more generous than in former years, because the angel of death had provided a decrease in his expenses.

When Ian Marshall asked permission to accept a dinner invitation, Algernon told him his time was his own and conveyed the offer from Lady Lucas. "Accept if you wish, but do not feel obliged. If you prefer, I think we can keep you here."

"I would much rather stay here." The new parson hesitated. "If I may, Sir, I have a gift for you."

Although Ian Marshall could not be said to have earned a gift by long and devoted service, Algernon had gifted him with a pound note. The unexpected present he received in return was a small volume of poems.

"You have been very kind to me, and I hope you enjoy it."

Algernon had declined invitations for the family to dine with neighbors and joined the two ladies at table. The goose was carved and enjoyed. The plum pudding was, as always, agreed to be the best ever tasted.

After dinner, Algernon went to his library and examined the books Elizabeth had sent him for Christmas. Selecting a promising novel, he was totally absorbed after reading only a few pages and was annoyed when the Lucases were announced. He had seen enough of them for one Christmas and carried his book with him into the drawing room.

"My dear friends," he said, smiling, "I had no hope of seeing you again today."

Lady Lucas did not bother with a preamble. "Mr. Bennet, please do not forget to tell Mr. Marshall we invited him to live at Lucas Lodge. So many people pestered him after service, we had no chance to invite him ourselves. It will not be fair if he accepts another offer," she said, indignant. "Our invitation should have been first."

"Trust me," Algernon said, casually placing the open book on the table at his elbow. He was tempted to say the invitation had already been declined. He could add that, in addition to his income as parson, Ian was heir to a fine estate, but Christmas was not the time to torment a devoted neighbor.

Observing the pursuit of a potential son-in-law was not a new experience for Algernon. When Bingley arrived in the neighborhood, Mrs. Bennet had been so ferocious in claiming him, she all but frightened him away. Despite her, Bingley and Jane managed to fall in love, dashing Lady Lucas's hopes of Bingley for *her* son-in-law. She did not intend to lose her chance at snaring Mr. Marshall.

Miss Pepper joined them, carrying a sewing box. Curtsying, she said, "If I may, I will work in here where the candles are brighter."

"Of course, my dear," Algernon said.

Miss Pepper and Lady Lucas fell into chatter about sewing. Algernon caught a few words while casting furtive glances at his book.

"Needlework...so beautiful...thought I would work...worn spots on the valances."

"Will you be here long enough to complete—"

Casually turning a page, Algernon chimed in. "Yes, indeed. What a good idea."

Lady Lucas stood up, waving her handkerchief. "Oh, my," she moaned.

"Lady Lucas, may I get you a sherry?" Without waiting for her answer, Miss Pepper rang the bell.

Lady Lucas stared at her, then turned to her husband. "We should—we must go."

Algernon escorted them to the door, and Lady Lucas said, "My dear Mr. Bennet, as your friend, I must remind you to remember dear Mrs. Bennet."

"A wife is a hard thing to forget."

"You were happily married for many years."

"We were married for many years."

Lady Lucas seemed agitated. "You would not want anything to tarnish the memory."

Mrs. Bennet was dead. Nothing *could* change the memory. Puzzled, Algernon said, "Lady Lucas, no matter what the future holds, I can never forget."

Lady Lucas gasped. "What the future holds!"

When the door closed behind them, Algernon snatched up his book and hurried back to the library. Leaning back in his favorite chair, he stretched one leg in front of him and propped the other on the footstool. Comfortable, he trusted he would not be interrupted again. He finished a chapter and was eagerly turning the page when it struck him.

When Elizabeth was at Longbourn, Algernon had teased Lady Lucas about wanting to remarry.

She had seen him holding Miss Pepper's waist in a way she might have misinterpreted.

What had they been talking about while he was sneaking glances at his book? Apparently Miss Pepper was doing a bit of mending, suggesting a personal interest in the household.

Poor Lady Lucas must have thought—the silly woman suspected—he and Miss Pepper had intentions. Surely, that was what her prattle was about. She was actually afraid he might marry again and tighten his grip on life, deliberately delaying her son-in-law's rightful possession of Longbourn.

He was stunned by the absurdity of anyone thinking marriage was a life extender. The idea of a second Mrs. Bennet was almost enough to send him to join the first. Lady Lucas had nothing to worry about.

Chapter 17

The book was long enough to keep him engrossed for several days. Only a few pages remained when Hill brought him a late Christmas greeting:

My dear Papa, Merry Christmas. We used your Christmas present to pay the market. We are very grateful for all your help. We will always be grateful when you help us.

Wickham gave me a bed for the baby. I knitted a scarf for him, but it did not turn out right. He said it could be a coverlet for the baby. Wickham does not want me to walk out alone. He is afraid I might slip and fall on the snow. He is again on good terms with his colonel and very busy. Your respectful and loving daughter, Lydia Wickham.

Lydia held an anxious spot in Algernon's mind, and he was comforted to hear Wickham's concern for his little family had not been fleeting. Hard as it was to believe, impending fatherhood might truly have tapped into his virtue. Perhaps Algernon could no longer boast of having one of England's worst rascals as a son-in-law.

Thinking about his visit with them, Algernon unrolled a large piece of drawing paper and arranged it on his desk, anchoring the corners with little paperweights. He usually drew in a sketchpad easily kept out of sight, but the picture looming in mind required a larger field. After mending his pens, he started to draw and soon lost track of time. He was surprised when shadows moved across his desk, and he had to light the candles.

After adding a few more strokes to the drawing, he sat back to appraise it. He was chuckling when Hill brought his tea. "Sir, an express arrived."

Algernon expected it to be from Elizabeth. It was not. He read it; stunned, he read it again:

My Dear Sir, It is my duty to inform you that your new parson is a common thief. Several times I suspected Mr. Ian Marshall had defrauded me by misrepresenting the amount of money he collected in tithes. However, I was too honorable to confront him. Now a matter has arisen which I cannot ignore.

Our church has long had in its possession a silver and ebony cross of unique design that may date from the reign of Henry VIII. The cross is so valuable, it was displayed only at Christmas and Easter. It did not adorn our altar this Christmas. It is missing, and Marshall is the only person who could have taken it. Although I am certain he can sell it for more than one hundred pounds, I will accept one hundred pounds to reimburse our church for the loss. To spare you embarrassment, I will delay going to the magistrate for one week. If we are properly compensated, I will not make the loss public. You will, of course, want to discharge Marshall immediately.

Sir, I remain your humble servant, etc., Robert Worthington

Algernon could hardly believe he was reading correctly. *Marshall a thief.* From the beginning of their acquaintance, Ian had gained his respect. Not only did he like the man, he had involved Mr. Hendrick when introducing him to the parish. Could he have made such a horrible error in judgment?

Tea would no longer do. He poured himself a brandy—apricot brandy. He had ordered a bottle for himself when he purchased some to send to Worthington. Now the brandy reminded him how much he had disliked the man. Worthington's manner was totally insincere, and he had not extended the common decency of allowing Marshall to officiate at Mr. Hendrick's funeral until promised a gift. He paid Marshall pitifully, yet had been furious when the young curate accepted a better post.

Though disturbed, Algernon assured himself he could trust his own judgment. Ian Marshall could not be a thief. Worthington had to be mistaken. Either someone else had taken the cross or it was misplaced. His drawing no longer intrigued him. His mind was elsewhere. He considered several courses of action and would not show Marshall the letter until he decided what to do.

At supper, he tried to maintain his usual manner with Marshall, but casual discourse was difficult. Leaving the table early, he retreated back to the library and was pouring himself another brandy when Miss Pepper appeared.

"I am returning *Ivanhoe*," she said, finding the book's place on the shelf. "It was very exciting."

She made no move to leave and, after a silence, said, "Mr. Bennet, can I be of help?"

Surprised, he looked at her. "There is nothing... it is nothing." She was presumptuous, but discerning. He had to admit it.

Miss Pepper selected another book and sat down without invitation. Turning pages, she spoke. "I felt something about Mr. Marshall disturbed you."

At most, he might have seemed grim and looked at Marshall too closely. The woman's perception left him unable to chastise her impudence. He even considered showing her the letter but decided he should not show it to anyone but Marshall.

"You may trust me never to betray a confidence." Looking up, she met his eye.

He hesitated, then handed her the letter. A long time passed as she studied it. Despite himself, he was anxious to know what she thought.

"I know Mr. Marshall has earned your good opinion," she began. "I doubt you bestow it very often. What is your opinion of Mr. Worthington?"

"Lazy, I think, and self-indulgent." Algernon's answer made him uneasy. "Of course, it does not mean he is dishonest or disreputable."

"Indeed not," she said, smiling unexpectedly. "Excellent men sometimes have a penchant for self-indulgence."

After a moment, she continued. "The night we arrived, Mr. Marshall told us his brother was the squire of a large estate in Warwickshire. I should imagine Mr. Worthington would know that."

"You are thinking that if I do not pay him, Mr. Worthington might expect the squire to come to his brother's rescue to protect the family name."

She nodded. "His suggesting a payment seems odd. He should want the cross returned."

"Then you think his assertion might be fraudulent?"

"You think so, too."

"I do, but…." He stopped.

"You cannot be certain."

"I *am* certain," Algernon said sharply, rejecting any doubt. "The allegation is either a deliberate lie or Mr. Worthington is mistaken."

"He allows only a week to resolve the matter."

"In the morning, I will show Mr. Marshall the letter. If he tells me he did not take the cross, I will believe him."

"What will you recommend he do?"

Algernon paced. "I do not know."

"Mr. Bennet, it may not be your decision." Miss Pepper leaned back, her arms resting limp on the sides of her chair.

Her presence was surprisingly calming, and he had to admit she was right. Ian Marshall should be told he had Algernon's confidence and then decide for himself how to respond.

Miss Pepper walked around the desk. Picking up a candle, she held it over his drawing. "The man leading the way has a chest on his back. The woman is carrying a basket. It must be moving day." She smiled. "Mr. Bennet, this is delightful." Turning back to the drawing, she said, "The man with the wheelbarrow looks older. Do you think he should be a little rounder in the middle?"

Algernon stood tall and pressed his hand to his waist. "No," he said emphatically.

Chapter 18

Algernon instructed the butler to send Mr. Marshall to the library as soon as he came downstairs. The young man soon appeared, looking very eager. If there was an assignment, he was ready to take it on.

Algernon did not waste time. "I received a very disturbing letter. It concerns you." Without further comment, he held out the letter. Marshall took it and, reading, his smile faded. Clutching the letter, he stared straight ahead and took breaths in deep, audible gulps.

"What do you have to say?" Algernon asked.

Ian Marshall struggled to speak. "His claims— his charges—are not true."

"You did not take the cross?"

Marshall crushed the letter in his hand. "No! And I never held back a farthing of his tithes."

"Did you ever see the cross?"

"Mr. Worthington had me polish the silver part before the service last Easter."

"Where was the cross the last time you saw it?"

Marshall shook his head. "I do not think I ever saw it after Easter."

"Could you have taken it? I mean, did you know where it was kept?"

"Yes."

The terse answer was more convincing to Algernon than a long explanation. "You need time to think and decide what you want to—"

"Mr. Bennet, I do not need time!" Marshall jerked to his feet, stood at the window for a brief moment, then spun around and faced Algernon. "I will go to Mr. Worthington immediately and tell him the cross must be misplaced. If he allows it, I will help him look for it."

"And if you do not find it?"

Marshall dropped back into the chair. "Then I will tell him—convince him—I have no idea what happened to it."

"What will you do if Worthington does not believe you?"

The color drained from Marshall's face, but his voice was firm. "I will stand my ground."

"Does Mr. Worthington know your brother has a large property in Warwickshire?"

"When I first went to work for him, I told him I grew up there."

"If I do not pay him, he may think your brother will pay to protect the family name."

Ian Marshall shrugged. "I doubt it. During all the months I was at Hamstone, I never received mail from Warwickshire. It was obvious I was not in touch with my brother."

"Mr. Worthington sounds more interested in money than the return of the cross," Algernon said, remembering Miss Pepper's comments.

"If it were not for his accusations," Marshall said, waving the letter, "I would not expose him, but Mr. Worthington is a greedy man." He stopped and seemed to reconsider. "But even so, he would not— I do not think he would make this claim—unless he believed it."

"If you cannot prove your innocence, will your brother assist you?"

Ian Marshall returned to the window and stood with his back to Algernon. "I would never ask for his help. I doubt he would give it if I did."

"An appeal from you in this matter might help heal the breach between you."

"The breach existed before I was born. My mother first went to Oakleigh to be my brother's governess. She was a fine musician, and her talent at the pianoforte was often called upon. My father loved to listen to her play, and they became friends. After his wife died, he did what all his relatives and friends thought was inexcusable—he married her."

Marshall could not stay still and moved from chair to window and back again. "Her father—my grandfather—was not a gentleman. He was an artisan renowned for building wonderful clocks. My mother was a sweet, lovely person, but my father never overcame the stigma of marrying beneath him. The family was disgraced. They did not deny me a gentleman's education, but they regarded my birth as a blot on the Marshall name."

"And now you and your brother have no contact with each other? He does not assist you at all?"

"He accepted his family's opinion and considers me undeserving. I have nothing against him. I wish we could have been friends."

He stopped pacing. "Mr. Bennet, I have the pound you were kind enough to give me. I can pay my fare to Hamstone and back. If I get to Meryton in time to get the post, I can go today."

"I think you should write first. Tell Worthington you know nothing about the cross and await his reply."

"I will go today," Ian Marshall said. "I have to face him and tell him he is wrong."

While admiring the young man's determination, Algernon was almost certain the trip was a mistake.

Despite misgivings, he ordered the carriage to hurry Marshall to Meryton. The coachman returned and reported they had been in time. Mr. Marshall had caught the post and was on his way to Hamstone.

Mary and Miss Pepper were paying calls, and the house was quiet, something Algernon usually appreciated. Today, he would have welcomed a little noise and almost wished Mary was home to attack the pianoforte. Almost wished, but not quite.

His apprehensions stayed with him all day and made it difficult for him to keep his mind on anything, even his new books. Although it was only three days since he had received Elizabeth's last letter, he decided to answer it. He risked setting a precedent for prompt replies, but writing to his favorite daughter would be a pleasant distraction. He began the letter with an account of Lady Lucas's worries about Miss Pepper becoming the future mistress of Longbourn, certain his Lizzy would enjoy the absurdity of it as much as he did:

Lizzy, the poor lady must actually be convinced marrying again would prolong my life. I daresay some men would vouchsafe marriage shortens the path to the grave.

He repeated an earlier promise to visit the Bingleys and meet his grandson in the spring. Then he thought about Mr. Marshall and remembered Elizabeth's particular inquiries about him for Miss

Darcy. It pleased him to tell her the parish had been delighted to welcome him. He also told her the competition to acquire him as a son-in-law was already intense.

Other information about Ian Marshall ran through his mind. *In addition to being very well liked, Mr. Marshall has been called a common thief and accused of stealing an expensive cross.*

He could hardly entrust such enchanting information to paper. He blotted the letter and put it away. He would finish it when Marshall returned.

Chapter 19

Three days later, the letter to Lizzy was still in the drawer. The newly installed parson of Longbourn church had neither returned nor sent word. Algernon was increasingly uneasy and, during his morning walk, was too preoccupied to enjoy the winter scene.

Miss Pepper was waiting when he returned to the house. "Mr. Bennet, I received this letter," she said, showing it to him. "My brother wants me to convey his gratitude for your great kindness to me."

Algernon stamped snow off his boots. "Where is your brother?"

"Andrew is in Portsmouth. He has received his commission and is awaiting assignment to a ship. It may not come for some time, so he plans to find lodgings." She looked down. "I enjoy my time at Longbourn. Indeed, this is a delightful place, but I do not want to overextend my visit. I think I should join him." Her sigh was audible.

"If you would like to remain here, you are welcome," Algernon said as the butler helped him remove his great coat. "In fact, I think you *should* stay," he added, thinking that when her brother went to sea, she would probably be alone in Portsmouth.

He realized he might have been too quick in extending her invitation, but her presence did create a great improvement in Mary, primarily by keeping her from shadowing him. She was no trouble—at least not much trouble—and there were times when he found her interesting to talk to.

"Mr. Bennet, I am so pleased that you invited me to remain at Longbourn, I almost forgot something. She hesitated. "I hope you will not think me presumptuous."

He raised his eyebrows. "You presumptuous?"

"Sir, if Mr. Marshall does not return today, we will have no one to take the service tomorrow. Do you not think we should get someone?"

"Today is Saturday," Algernon said, realizing.

"Indeed, and tomorrow is Sunday."

"An astute deduction."

"I have a suggestion," she said, missing the little sarcasm.

The housemaid was coming down the stairs, her arms laden with soiled linen. Despite the load, she managed a polite curtsy before hurrying toward the laundry room.

"Are not the servants instructed to use the back staircase?" Miss Pepper asked.

"I suppose," Algernon said. "They always did before...." He paused, suddenly aware that before and after were measured by his wife's death. "I do not take an interest in those things," he said briskly.

"You may want to remind them. When only the family is here, I daresay it does not matter, but you will want more formality when you have guests."

"I will speak to Hill about it. Now let me hear your suggestion."

"First, do you not want your tea?" she said, following him into the library and ringing the bell. She righted a book that had fallen over. "Yesterday, Mary and I took the carriage into Meryton and—"

"I know," Algernon said, interrupting. "The coachman must have been delighted to hitch the horses and warm the carriage for such a short ride."

"Indeed he was. While we were shopping, we let him tend his own business. At the milliner's Mary purchased a most attractive bonnet with—"

"I am not interested in women's fashions," Algernon said, interrupting again.

"Mrs. Baxter, the milliner, mentioned that her neighbor has a nephew visiting for the holidays. And what do you think?"

"He makes hats, too."

"He is newly in orders and has no assignment. Mrs. Baxter thinks he would be pleased to serve wherever he might be needed."

Sarah carried in the tea tray. Miss Pepper filled Algernon's cup and added the speck of cream he required. "He is Mr. John Allen. I told Mrs. Baxter you might need him. She will mention it, and he will not be surprised if he hears from you."

In his concerns for Ian Marshall, getting a replacement had never occurred to him, not that it mattered. The non-presumptuous Miss Pepper had gone to town to make inquiries unless, of course, the milliner had most fortuitously mentioned her neighbor's nephew. "I assume you know the man's address," he said.

"I do," she answered, pouring tea for herself. "Mr. Allen is staying with his aunt in the cottage next to the shop."

Algernon was not about to open his inkbottle immediately. Instead, he behaved as if he were giving the matter consideration. "I am not certain. After all, what do we know about Mr. Allen?" he asked, deliberately sounding skeptical.

"We know he is a clergyman."

Algernon opened the inkbottle. As he wrote, he commented, "Mr. Marshall is very well-liked. His absence will be a disappointment."

"To some more than others. Mr. Bennet, do you think knowing he has been accused of theft would discourage Lady Lucas?"

Startled, Algernon looked at her. Her perception did not match his own, but there was no denying she had a certain cleverness.

"My dear Miss Pepper," he said, amused, "I do not think anything would discourage Lady Lucas."

A smile played at her mouth. "Perhaps you are right. When a woman has determined on a man for a daughter or, I might say, even for herself, she is usually very hard to discourage." She set her cup down, dropped a deep curtsy, and left.

He sent the letter to John Allen, and the coach-man returned with an eager acceptance. Miss Pepper was right. Any clergyman would do for one Sunday, and he was amused at her pretense of accidentally hearing that one was available.

The next morning, Mr. Allen stepped behind the Longbourn church pulpit. He was tall—older than Algernon would have expected for a man recently in orders—and the most noticeable thing about his appearance was bright red hair. Algernon's own hair had once been equally bright, but fortunately he had never shared the eccentricities often found in red-haired people.

Although Algernon always hurried away after church, he rarely managed to escape without a robust exchange of greetings. Today, people lagged behind. Several seemed to avoid looking his way. Greetings were muted. Strangest of all, no one asked about Ian Marshall's absence.

Chapter 20

Nothing could spread faster than a rumor about a clergyman, and surely a rumor about Ian Marshall was in the wind. Algernon did not investigate what was being said. Information embellished by many retellings would be useless as fact and annoying as fiction.

Algernon paid Mr. Allen the courtesy of inviting him to dinner. Mary and Miss Pepper would provide enough, and more than enough, conversation for a sociable meal, and he did not join them. The inspiration to be sociable struck only occasionally, and this was not one of its moments.

The next morning, he ordered the carriage and set out for Hamstone. Gloom was the color of the day. The sky was not so much overcast as lifeless. The terrain was equally depressing. Algernon did not bother selecting scenes to draw.

At their earlier encounter, Mr. Worthington had greeted him like an old friend. This time, when Algernon was shown into the sitting room, he was received more like a brother.

"Mr. Bennet! Mr. Bennet!" Worthington repeated. "How nice to see you."

The man had to realize Algernon's visit related to Ian Marshall, not quite the basis for a pleasant encounter, but Algernon played his part. Smiling, he gave Worthington's hand a hearty shake. "Seeing you certainly suits the mood of the day."

"Sir, I am greatly grieved about Mr. Marshall," Worthington said, his smile crumbling to a properly downcast expression. "Who would suspect a man of the cloth of being a criminal?"

"I am afraid in this matter one is forced to suspect a man of the cloth," Algernon said. He doubted Worthington's great grief had jaded his appetite. The few steps he took demonstrated a walk that would catch the eye of a duck. His neck bulged thick above his clerical bib.

Algernon accepted a sherry, sat back in a chair and crossed his legs. On his first visit, he had paid no attention to the parsonage. Now his need to evaluate Worthington made everything pertinent. Looking around, he decided the furniture was French. A mahogany, elaborately carved, long-case clock stood in the entry hall. Although not the equal to the clock at Pemberley, it was impressive. The fine tapestries—everything in the room—declared that either Mr. Worthington or his wife had a taste for elegance. Algernon wondered if they had the income to support it.

Sipping the sherry gave him a moment to plan an approach, and he decided to coax Worthington down the path to truth. "My dear sir," he began, "I do not know that Marshall *is* a criminal. That is something you need to explain to me."

Worthington gave an airy wave of his arm. "My letter explained it."

"You wrote about a missing cross. Sorry, but I must trouble you for the details."

Worthington plopped into a huge, cushioned chair that clashed with the refinement of the room. "The details are simple. The church has long owned a priceless cross. When he left, Marshall stole it."

Algernon noted that the expensive cross of Worthington's letter had gained a promotion to priceless. "Are you saying no one else had access to the church, not even the people who clean there?"

Worthington shook his head. "The cross was so valuable, I kept it in the house."

"Surely, your housekeeper and other servants knew where it was."

Worthington tipped his head back, an arrogant gesture. "My servants have been with me a long time and are very faithful. I would gladly trust my housekeeper, Mrs. Jennings, with my life."

"Splendid," Algernon said, wondering what Mrs. Jennings would do if his life fell into her keeping. He set his glass down. "Marshall has not returned to Longbourn. Do you know where he is?"

"Mr. Bennet, you do not know?" Startled, the big man bulged forward in his chair "I thought surely you had heard. I thought you had to know."

"Know what?" Algernon demanded.

Leaning back again, Worthington composed himself. "It is my unhappy duty to tell you that Mr. Ian Marshall has been taken up by the magistrate. He is in jail."

Algernon was stunned. The gossip had been about more than accusations. Longbourn's new parson was in jail. "What is the charge?" he asked, his voice sharp.

"My dear Mr. Bennet, the charge is the theft of the Hamstone church cross."

"The magistrate could not take him up simply because you think he is responsible for a missing cross. You have no proof."

"To the contrary, I do have proof. A maid saw Mr. Marshall put the cross into his valise."

"You did not say that in your letter."

Worthington smiled benignly. "I think you must agree that the less said about the matter, the better."

"I do not agree. Will you be kind enough to let me talk to the maid?"

Worthington's smile froze. "Why do you want to talk to her?

"To decide whether I think she is telling the truth."

"I assure you I have perfect confidence in her truthfulness."

"Excellent. After I talk to her, perhaps I will."

"She has already told the magistrate everything and—"

"What is her name?"

"There is no point going into that." Worthington's sounded exasperated. Their brotherhood was waning.

"In your letter, you said we had a week to settle the matter, yet you did not wait." Algernon paused. "Am I correct in thinking you suggested a solution? I believe a sum of money."

Worthington shrugged, an indifferent gesture. Surely, he had never given money a thought. "Mr. Bennet, I am sympathetic to your situation and realize it would be an embarrassment to have it known that the parson of your church is dishonest. Perhaps it is not too late to make amends."

"Ian Marshall was parson of Longbourn church for one week. He was your curate for ten months and quite well paid, I understand." Algernon was not ready to antagonize Worthington, but the words jumped out.

Worthington did not notice. "Indeed, he was my curate for some months. That is why I feel a loyalty to him, despite the inconsiderate way he left me."

"A loyalty to him?" Algernon was incredulous. Worthington did not seem dismayed that his former curate was in jail. To the contrary, he looked smug. Whatever else his motives, Worthington wanted the man punished for daring to leave him.

"If the church were compensated for the loss, I could consider withdrawing the charge. Perhaps an adjustment could be found that would clear his name."

"Your letter set the price of the cross at one hundred pounds," Algernon said, wondering what adjustment could be made to clear the name of a man accused of theft.

"I assure you the cross was worth much more than one hundred pounds. I have to inquire; I have to wait."

"To see if the cross can be located?" More and more, Algernon shared Miss Pepper's suspicions about why Worthington showed no interest in recovering the cross he now called priceless.

"Marshall will never tell us what he did with it. I grieve to have to tell you, but he lied repeatedly, insisting he had never seen it."

Algernon rarely got angry. Few things in life were worth that much exertion, but now he felt a growing rage. Standing up, he said, "Mr. Marshall told me he cleaned the cross at Easter. I do not believe he told you he had never seen it."

Worthington looked cornered, then donned his beneficent smile. "Ah, that is true. He did have the decency to admit he cleaned the cross. That must have been when he realized how valuable it is."

The clock chimed, then struck twelve. During the unavoidable pause in conversation, Algernon studied Worthington. The man was not mistaken. He was lying. Marshall had not stolen the Hamstone church cross, and Robert Worthington knew it.

Suddenly, there was another din, this time not the clock. Angry shrieks rang and a snarling voice issued commands. Mr. Worthington withered if a man his size could be said to wither. "My wife has returned. Apparently, she has a complaint with one of the servants."

"One would think so," Algernon said as the shrieks got louder. For Worthington's sake, he hoped the nasty voice was in close keeping with the lady's other charms.

"Mr. Worthington, do we agree that if I pay you one hundred pounds, you will cancel your complaint?" Algernon had no intention of paying him but wanted to hear Worthington name his price.

Without answering, Worthington pulled himself out of his chair. "Mr. Bennet, I have a most pressing appointment. I shall write to you, and we can decide this matter another time."

Chapter 21

Algernon had managed to save Lydia and Wickham from imprisonment. Now his task was more difficult. Ian was already jailed. Algernon had to get him out. Perhaps the young man did not have the claim to his loyalty that Lydia did, but Algernon had praised him to Longbourn church. He would stand by his words.

He went to the Hamstone jail, a tiny, stone structure that looked old enough to date to the Roman occupation. Below the lone window, a pile of rocks and bricks formed little stairs, likely constructed by children to allow them to peer inside. With most town jails, the object of such attention was apt to be an unruly villager who would be released when he could walk without meandering sideways. Today, the jail had neither an occupant nor a jailer.

His next went to the magistrate's office, where he was told that Ian Marshall had been in Hamstone jail but had been transferred to the county jail to await court. A trip to the county jail would take him miles farther from Longbourn. Algernon looked at his watch. It would be very late when he got home, but there was no decision to make.

The short winter day was slipping into twilight when he reached the jail, a small building with an unadorned, gray stone exterior sufficiently depressing to discourage people from crime.

The old jailer scoffed at his request to see Mr. Marshall. "Obediah Dopple says it is past the time to be bringing prisoners up here."

"May I speak to Mr. Dopple?"

"Aye, you are speaking to him."

Algernon held up a shilling. "Algernon Bennet says perhaps it is not too late."

Mr. Obediah Dopple whisked the shilling out of Algernon's hand. "I kin let you go downstairs."

Carrying a candle, he led the way down several narrow stairs to a large, low-ceilinged room where the musty air hung heavy with oppressive smells. Algernon caught his breath, then looked around. Several people, little more than shadows in the dim light, sat on benches against the wall.

"For a ha'penny you can use m'candle, but you kin nay stay down here long."

Not having a ha'penny, Algernon gave him a penny, accepted the candle, and looked around.

One of the shadows called out. "Mr. Bennet!"

Algernon held the candle toward the sound and was stunned when Ian Marshall came toward him. The young man could not have lost significant weight in such short time, yet he looked thinner. Usually clean-shaven, he had the start of a black beard. It did not make him appear older. Somehow it made him look younger.

"For God's sake, why did you not let me know where you were?"

"Sir, I hoped—God, I prayed—no one would find out." In a despairing voice, he asked, "Do other people know?"

"I am afraid so," Algernon said, not wanting to tell him that he himself was probably the last person in the county to hear.

"I am so ashamed."

"Ashamed?" Algernon bellowed. "You should not be ashamed. Angry yes! Mr. Worthington is a scoundrel. That liar should be here, not you." He felt more emotion than he had ever known in his life. He trembled, torn between rage at Worthington and concern for Marshall.

"I should have tried to get word to you. I know that. But there is someone...someone I hoped would never know. Not that it can ever matter now."

"Your brother?"

"Not my brother. A person not exactly at Longbourn, but—" He stopped. "I have no right to mention it."

Algernon did not need his keen awareness to understand; Marshall would suffer alone if it would keep Georgiana Darcy from knowing where he was.

They moved to stand beneath a high, narrow window where the last thread of daylight blended with the dim candle glow. "Ian, Mr. Worthington told me a maid saw you put the cross in your valise."

"It is not true!"

"I believe you."

"Thank you...your opinion...a comfort. More than I can say." His voice choked.

"Could the maid have stolen the cross?"

Ian shook his head. "Bridget is terrified and will say what Mr. Worthington tells her to say. But he would not have sent for the magistrate if Mrs. Worthington had not made him do it."

Algernon cupped a hand around the flickering candle, shielding it from a draft. He was puzzled. "Why did she want the magistrate? Worthington claimed he wanted payment to avoid a scandal, but now, with you in jail—" He stopped, not wanting to say the scandal might already have reached all the way to London.

"I told Mr. Worthington I knew nothing about his missing cross. I swore I never held back his tithes. He would not listen. I got angry and accused him of lying. I was shouting, and that is when Mrs. Worthington came and—"

"She insisted on sending for the magistrate," Algernon said, finishing for him. It was clear now. Mrs. Worthington believed her husband's accusations and, in righteous belligerence, had screamed for the magistrate. Robert Worthington had been caught between his wife and a lie. After hearing the woman rant, Algernon had no doubt Worthington felt safer with the lie and had intimidated a maid to confirm his story.

Earlier, Algernon had rejected the thought of paying Worthington, but conditions in the jail were miserable; the dark winter nights would seem endless. He could not leave Marshall there. "Worthington wants money, and I think he will settle for a hundred pounds to drop the charge. I can pay him and debit it from your salary."

"That is good of you but—" Ian shook his head. "I did not steal anything. Paying him to drop the charge would be the same as saying I did. I could never be parson at Longbourn or serve in any other church. I would never be regarded as an honest man. I have to prove I am innocent when I am called to court."

"That might be months away," Algernon said. "Recently, I read about a case in Bath—"

"Mrs. Leigh-Perrot," Ian said. "They talk about her here. She was a gentlewoman accused of stealing black lace found wrapped in a package of white lace she had just purchased."

"I do not know how long she was in jail, but—"

"Eight months," Ian told him. "In court, it was proved the store's claim was a deliberate fraud."

"An accused person should have the right to be called to court promptly and not have to linger—" Algernon broke off at the sound of someone thumping down the stairs. It was a woman carrying a cooking pot. A shadowy figure rose from a bench and went to her.

"She is his wife," Ian said. "She brings his supper every night."

"They must feed you."

"One has to be very hungry to eat."

Ian knew he might have to spend many months in the misery of the jail, yet he refused ransom. Algernon wondered if, in similar circumstances, he could refuse relief and honored the man's courage.

After the woman gave her husband the pot, Algernon called her over and asked her name.

"I am Mrs. Logan." Her face was withered, her frame skeletal, and huge shoes, either accommodating very large feet or intended for a different owner, stuck out under a ragged dress. A threadbare shawl was apparently her only protection against the winter cold.

"Why is your husband here?" Algernon asked, trying to decide if she could be trusted.

"Sir, he is a good man, but he can nay pay the bank the money he borrowed for the thatcher who repaired our roof against the winter."

A debtor, Algernon thought, wondering at the sense of keeping a man in prison where he had no chance of earning money to repay what he owed.

"Mrs. Logan, I will pay you to bring my friend supper." He took out a half crown and held it for her to see. She stared but did not snatch.

"Aye, Sir, I will be more than glad to bring the young man his supper."

Algernon handed her the coin. "If you take good care of him, you will be well paid."

"I will not be allowed to bring him supper this night, but tomorrow he will have good beef soup and fresh bread."

"I think our good jailer will let you bring him something tonight," Algernon said, planning his next bribe.

There was a banging upstairs. "Obediah Dopple says ye kin both get up here now or ye can spend the night."

"That fellow likes to hear his own name."

"Mr. Bennet, we hear it all day. If it were my name, I would be slow to mention it," Ian said, smiling.

It impressed Algernon to realize imprisonment had not jaded the man's ability to be amused. He dug into his money belt and found four shillings and a half-crown. "I hope Mrs. Logan feeds you well."

Accepting the coins, Ian said, "Mr. Bennet, you called me your friend. Certainly, no man ever had a better one." He extended his hand.

Algernon enclosed it in both of his. "I am proud of you for standing up to Worthington. I promise to do everything I can to get you out of here soon."

Soon—but there was something he could do for him now.

He would never betray a confidence, especially one with Elizabeth, but under the circumstances, she would want him to give Ian a little pleasure. "Perhaps it will interest you to know," he said, before starting up the stairs, "my daughter Elizabeth received a letter from Miss Georgiana Darcy asking about you. I would say you managed to impress her quite favorably."

This time Ian Marshall's smile was no surprise.

Chapter 22

On the long ride home, Algernon worried he had made a promise he could not keep— but he *had* to keep it. He had to find a way to prove Ian Marshall was innocent. It had been a long, disheartening day, but consolation awaited him at home.

"Lizzy!" He pulled her into an embrace.

"It was my turn to surprise you, but Miss Pepper said you had gone to Hamstone because of something related to Mr. Marshall. I am eager to meet him."

"A meeting has to be postponed for a while," he said dryly. He had never told anyone where he was going. Miss Pepper certainly had a talent for discerning other people's business.

When the family gathered at table for a late supper, Darcy told Mary the Pemberley library had seemed dejected since she left. "I am sure it feels your absence," he said. No doubt he wanted to please her, but he had to be amused. It was not the first time Algernon realized life with Elizabeth had lightened his character.

"I miss the library," Mary said. "However, I am certain it does not miss me. Libraries, indeed any place, can have an ambiance either happy or sad, but people, not places, experience the feelings. The mood in a beautiful garden is apt to be happy, and I should think the mood in a jail would be sad, because the prisoners are sad."

Suddenly, Algernon was transported back to a dank, odorous cellar.

"Mr. Bennet, Mr. and Mrs. Collins are visiting from Kent and called on you this morning," Miss Pepper said.

"I am sorry I missed Charlotte," Elizabeth said. "Did she have her little boy with her?"

Miss Pepper shook her head. "They will bring him when they call tomorrow."

"I hope you are not saying we have their return visit to look forward to," Algernon said, pulling himself back to the moment.

"Papa! I want to see Charlotte, and I will keep Mr. Collins out of your way."

"This is their second visit in a fortnight," Mary said. "The heartfelt call of home must be very tugging to bring them back to Hertfordshire so soon."

"Mary, Hertfordshire was never Mr. Collins' home." Algernon raised his wine glass high. "May I delay its becoming so for as long as possible."

"Such a quick return is surprising," Elizabeth said. "I remember Charlotte saying they could not afford frequent visits."

"I understand Mr. Collins is heir to this estate."

"I think Miss Pepper has found the reason for the frequent visits. He comes to count his trees." Algernon held up his wine glass again. "To dear Mr. Collins!"

Basking in Elizabeth's company, he enjoyed what remained of the evening and went up to his bedroom in a better mood than he had known during the day.

"Father, may I talk to you?"

"Of course, Lizzy," he said, opening the door at her knock.

When she stepped inside, her cheerful demeanor was gone. "Father, when Mary mentioned jails, you looked distressed. Did your reaction have anything to do with Mr. Marshall?"

Miss Pepper had known he went to Hamstone. Elizabeth realized the mention of jails disturbed him. How could a man maintain his privacy when surrounded by women?

When he did not answer promptly, she said, "I heard the maids talking. It sounded as if Mr. Marshall was in trouble. In fact—" She hesitated. "There is a report—a rumor—he is in jail."

Sitting down on the edge of his bed, he waved her to the chair. He had never finished her letter and now explained all the details of Worthington's accusations: "So I am afraid it is true. Worthington was furious with Marshall and thought of a way to get paid for punishing him. Now that Mr. Marshall has been accused publicly and the family name is involved, I would not be surprised if Worthington contacts his brother, hoping for a larger payment than he wanted from me."

"Father, it is an outrageous accusation for Mr. Worthington to make if he knows it is not true. Could he simply be mistaken? Or," she hesitated, "is it possible Mr. Marshall did steal the cross?"

Algernon gave his head a violent shake. "It is ridiculous to think an intelligent man would allow a maid to witness him packing an expensive item he was stealing."

"You dislike Mr. Worthington and you like Mr. Marshall."

"Are you thinking my judgment is impaired?"

"Of course not, Father, but you are not always aware—" She broke off abruptly and then said, "I understand Mr. Marshall is quite a charmer."

"You certainly cannot think he charmed me."

"He charmed someone."

"Miss Darcy." It was a statement, not a query.

"We came because Georgiana wrote and asked if we would meet her at Longbourn to accompany her back to Pemberley. I have no doubt seeing Mr. Marshall was in her thoughts."

"Even before this trouble, Darcy could not have been pleased with his sister's interest in him."

Elizabeth shook her head. "He does not know."

She had always valued candor, and Algernon was surprised she was keeping something from her husband. Seeming to read his thoughts, she said, "I cannot betray Georgiana's confidence. It is up to her to tell her brother."

"Georgiana's interest in Marshall is very much reciprocated." Algernon took her hand. "He acted brave, but he has to be suffering. Lizzy, I wanted to do something, say something, to lighten his spirits, and I betrayed your confidence."

"You told him Georgiana asked me about him."

"Lizzy, he was so dejected."

She squeezed the hand that held hers. "I am glad you told him."

"He has a gentleman's background; he is intelligent, pleasant company, and certainly not one to put on airs, but—" Algernon shook his head. "There can be no point in pursuing that now."

"Pursuing what?"

"Nothing," he said quickly.

"I think you were planning to promote a romantic attachment between Georgiana and Mr. Marshall."

"Never! I am not a person to concern myself with other people's matrimonial intentions."

"You *should* be," she said emphatically.

"It is no matter now. When Miss Darcy finds out Mr. Marshall is in jail, it will douse the fame."

"She has a very susceptible heart and will want to believe he is innocent."

"He *is* innocent. You have to decide for yourself whether to tell her I think so."

"She is a dear girl, and I know she will suffer."

"Perhaps Colonel Fitzwilliam will help heal the wound. If I am not mistaken, he has more than a cousinly interest in the lady."

"You are quite perceptive, at least," she said slowly, "about that situation. But it is over. The colonel spoke to Darcy who discouraged him. Not that it mattered. When she learned of his interest in her, Georgiana insisted she loved him as a cousin and never would in any other way."

"Since Darcy disobliged Lady Catherine de Bough by marrying you, perhaps now Colonel Fitzwilliam will feel an inclination to fall properly in love with cousin Miss de Bough and her fortune."

Elizabeth smiled. "Oh yes, Lady Catherine did insist I refuse Darcy. Strangely, she thought then he would want to marry her daughter. If she now has the colonel in her sights, the poor lady can expect more disappointment."

"What evil awaits her this time?"

"Fitzwilliam visited the Bingleys and renewed his acquaintance with Bingley's sister, Caroline. Unless dear Jane is mistaken, we will soon hear of their engagement."

"Lizzy, I am sure your sister would not mistake a meeting of hearts—or fortunes—under her own roof."

"One should always be aware of what is taking place under one's roof. Father, how do you and Miss Pepper get on?"

The change in topic surprised him. "What do you mean?"

"She did not impress you at Pemberley."

"I judged her a little harshly. She is not a stupid woman, and she has worked some improvement in Mary." He smiled. "I must say, on occasion, she has unwittingly been very helpful."

"Unwittingly," Elizabeth repeated, "She spoke of an alteration she thought was needed in the breakfast parlor. Did she mention it to you?"

"Do you mean rearranging the cabinetry to let in more daylight? The idea is quite perceptive."

"Father, perception is essential. Without it, we might end up in situations we did not foresee."

"Very possible, my dear, very possible."

Going to the door, she stood motionless. He waited, thinking she was about to tell him something.

"Good night, Father." She gave her head an odd shake and closed the door behind her.

Chapter 23

When the family was at breakfast, Mrs. Hendrick was announced. She paused in the doorway. "Mr. Bennet," she said, "I am sorry to interrupt, but the carriage has arrived. I cannot take my leave without telling you how grateful I am for your wonderful kindnesses to us."

Jumping up, Elizabeth held out both hands to her. "Mrs. Hendrick, are we losing you?"

Algernon was about to echo the same question when he remembered she had told him her son wanted her to live with him and his family. He had never realized a move was imminent. Before he could wish her good journey and happy in her new home, she thanked him, not once but many times, for his generosity through the years.

Algernon could recall only a few routine acts that could hardly be called more than neighborly.

"Mrs. Hendrick, you and your husband were very deserving. I wish—I *should*—have done more."

After she had said her farewells and received a kiss from Elizabeth, Algernon put his arm around her frail shoulders and accompanied her to the door. He watched as she made her way down the lane.

Miss Pepper joined him. "A dear lady," she said. "I am certain she and her husband served you and the parish well."

Algernon nodded. "I am afraid they did."

"I have no doubt you were kinder to her than you think, and I am sure the generosity she appreciated will continue when you send her a stipend each year."

Algernon stopped. *How could he have failed to give her money now and the assurance of an annual stipend?*

He would have thought of it later and made amends, but this was the proper time. He rushed to get his money belt and, without putting on his coat, rushed out the door. "Mrs. Hendrick!"

Neighbors were presenting farewell gifts and helping load her possessions into the carriage. Algernon gave her two ten-pound notes and promised an annual gift. Watching the carriage head toward the road, he was glad to have acted in time. Occasionally, Miss Pepper proved useful, and he was almost tempted to thank her.

It was hard to put Ian Marshall out of mind, but returning to the house, he decided to try to enjoy Elizabeth's company. Unfortunately, the threatened return visit of Mr. Collins materialized early.

After a lengthy apology for the intrusion, Mr. Collins added, "I pride myself that because of our family connection and my dear Charlotte's friendship with Cousin Elizabeth, the intrusion is no less enjoyable than necessary."

Charlotte proudly produced the biped, and Elizabeth succumbed to feminine behavior, fussing over him and pronouncing him a darling little boy. Algernon could do no better than escape his guests by going outdoors. He had on his high boots, greatcoat, and was arranging his muffler when Mr. Collins accosted him in the entry.

"My dear Mr. Bennet, are you going out?"

'No, Sir, I thought I would dress against the draft in the drawing room."

"There is a blazing fire in the drawing room," Collins said, his interest clearly perked. "You must be quite ill."

"I am sorry to disappoint you," Algernon said, regretting the waste of good sarcasm. "I am going for a walk."

"May I offer to accompany you?"

"You may, but I will be forced to decline. I cannot deprive my other guests of your presence."

The butler was hurrying to open the door. Algernon reached it first, opened it and, taking great strides, headed toward the woods.

The sun shone through a scattering of clouds. The air had the crisp, fresh smell Algernon loved. He felt invigorated and tramping briskly, left deep footprints in the snow. He did not head home until he was certain Mr. Collins and his dear Charlotte would be gone. He was wrong.

"We return to Kent on Wednesday and may not see you again," Charlotte said when he put in an appearance. "We could not take our leave without saying goodbye."

"Hardly," Algernon said.

The darling little boy was ensconced on Elizabeth's lap, playing with the amber beads around her neck. She stopped attending him long enough to give Algernon a look.

"Hardly time enough for a good visit," Algernon said quickly.

Now they could render their goodbyes and leave, but Mrs. Collins remained seated. Mr. Collins turned to Algernon. "I think you and I should have a private discourse."

Algernon did not want a discourse with Collins, private or otherwise, and was framing his answer when Hill announced yet another guest. "Mr. John Allen," she said, showing him into the room.

Algernon had seen the man only once and, with all the distractions of late, would have had a hard time remembering him if it had not been for the red hair. "Mr. Allen," he said, standing up.

"Sir, I apologize for—"

Algernon interrupted. "No more apologies, if you please. I am glad to have the opportunity to ask if you will again be available for Sunday service."

"With pleasure, if you need me."

Mr. Collins stepped forward, and Algernon introduced Mr. Allen to him and the ladies.

"A clergyman," Mr. Collins said, giving Allen's hand a hardy shake. "My own parish is in Kent. Lady Catherine de Bough of Rosings Park is my esteemed patroness," he said grandly.

Mr. Allen looked properly impressed and, seeming pleased with each other, the two men fell into animated chatter. Algernon relished introducing clergymen to each other. It was almost as gratifying as putting two oxen under a common yoke.

Miss Pepper appeared carrying her sewing basket, and Mr. Collins was no longer Mr. Allen's interest. His total attention riveted on her. "Miss Pepper," he said, smiling, "I brought a book I think you will enjoy." He held out a volume bound in red. "It is a collection of sermons."

"It sounds more exciting than Sir Walter's *Ivanhoe*," Algernon said.

Smiling, Miss Pepper accepted the volume. "Probably not more exciting than *Ivanhoe,* but I look forward to reading it."

"Mr. Bennet, perhaps you and I can have our discourse now."

"I would rather have tea," Algernon said.

Mr. Collins seemed not to have heard and went toward the library. Algernon gave Elizabeth a commanding look. She was not to leave them alone.

As soon as the library door closed behind them, Mr. Collins began talking, a rambling chatter that did not hold Algernon's attention.

"Mr. Bennet, at your age, you must not consider altering your way of life. Shocks from such changes have been known to carry people off."

"It happens all the time," Algernon said, absently.

"What happens all the time?"

"Whatever you were talking about."

"I was talking about people who alter their way of life after youth has ceased to be their companion. The constant recollection of blessed Mrs. Bennet and your splendid family of five daughters—only the youngest of whom ever disgraced you—should keep you from considering such a thing. You must remember Mrs. Bennet."

"Mrs. Bennet?" Algernon asked, puzzled. He had been glancing at a pile of mail and wondering how much longer he could delay writing answers. Now he leaned back in his chair and gave Mr. Collins attention.

Standing up, Mr. Collins stretched as tall as his modest height would allow and assumed a pompous attitude his congregants undoubtedly encountered when he took the pulpit. "My esteemed cousin," he began, "it has been brought to my notice that you are contemplating a most serious step. I have come to warn you against it. You are the proud and blessed father of five daughters and though, as I mentioned, one of your daughters disgraced your family, we must also remember another daughter bestowed glorious honor on all the Bennets by marrying the nephew of Lady Catherine de Bough."

Algernon did not need to be reminded once, let alone twice, that Lydia had lived with Wickham before their marriage. Containing himself, his only response was, "Sir, my daughter Elizabeth honored Mr. Darcy by becoming his wife."

Collins kept babbling about how their five daughters and the memory of the revered, late Mrs. Bennet should be sufficient family for any man. "Truly, you should realize it would be unwise for you to do anything that might extend your familial obligations."

Suddenly, what Collins was saying made sense, or at least as much sense as the man was capable of.

Algernon was nothing short of staggered, realizing Mr. Collins and his in-laws were not worried a second marriage would tighten his hold on life. They were afraid a second Mrs. Bennet might do what the first had failed to do—extend his familial obligations by producing a male heir—and they feared Miss Pepper might become the mother of the loathsome child.

There was a knock on the door. "Father, I think you should—"

"Not now, Elizabeth." The shock was wearing off, and this had become a discourse Algernon intended to finish.

"Because of our relationship and my station in life, I must caution you on both practical and moral grounds."

"Moral grounds? Sir, I find this very serious indeed. Please, tell me exactly what immoral act you think I may be contemplating." Algernon was intrigued, wondering how direct Collins could bring himself to be.

The man had a rare talent for the obsequious and had once bragged about preparing little compliments to sprinkle into ordinary conversation. When he was not giving compliments, he liked to give speeches, usually garbled enough to impress Mary. Unfortunately, he had not prepared a speech in response to Algernon's blunt inquiry. He looked uneasy. "I think you know. I mean, she is living here at Longbourn and is involved in domestic improvements."

"Hill has been our housekeeper for many years, but if she is morally objectionable, I will dismiss her and ask Miss Pepper to select a replacement."

"No! Do not replace Hill. Do not ask Miss Pepper anything. Keep things just the way they are and remember Mrs. Bennet." After stuttering vague answers to a few more of Algernon's questions, he escaped out the door.

Algernon had to decide whether to be angry or amused at their fears that he might yet father a son, although youth was no longer his companion. Rubbing his chin, he remembered he had been angry at Worthington, and frequent bouts of anger required too much effort. He would be amused. With a little ingenuity, he could be very amused and perhaps enjoy a distraction from concerns about Ian Marshall.

Chapter 24

On Thursday, the sun made a bold appearance for mid-winter; the wind quieted, and
Elizabeth, Mary, and Miss Pepper took
advantage by venturing a walk to Meryton. With the
ladies away, Algernon challenged Darcy to a chess
game. An accomplished player, he looked forward
to besting his son-in-law.

Something went wrong. He did not recognize
Darcy's mode of attack and found himself facing
checkmate in only two more moves. Although not
usually eager for visitors, he brightened at the sound
of a carriage. With no way to save the king, he
delayed moving his doomed bishop until the butler
presented a card. He was amazed when he saw the
name written in embossed, silver letters:

*Alexander Marshall, Esquire, of Oakleigh in
Warwickshire.*

Darcy and Algernon both rose to acknowledge a tall, well-built man. Before responding to Algernon's greeting, he looked around, clearly assessing his surroundings. "Mr. Bennet," he said, extending his hand, "I am here about a very serious matter."

"Sir, we can talk in the library. First, allow me to introduce my son-in-law, Mr. Darcy."

As the two men shook hands, Algernon hurried the chess pieces back in the case.

"Darcy." Mr. Marshall repeated the name. "Are you from Derbyshire?"

When Darcy nodded acknowledgment, Alexander Marshall said, "I understand Pemberley is the largest estate in Derbyshire and belongs to the Darcy family."

"It has been in our family for many generations," Darcy said, pride edging his voice.

"May I ask who is master now?"

"I am."

Mr. Marshall's eyes widened, and he looked impressed. "An honor to meet you. My own estate is in Warwickshire. Perhaps you have heard of Oakleigh. It is considered one of the best wool producers in England." He paused. "I daresay not as important in wool production as Pemberley."

"Wool production at Pemberley has been very heavy. Recently my steward suggested selling one or two of our flocks."

"Our flocks are all prized. I would never consider selling."

Algernon was ready to be entertained by two men in verbal combat over their estates. He hoped they would get to counting sheep. Unfortunately, Darcy was no braggart. Smiling, he said, "With such fine sheep, it is no wonder you have excellent wool production."

With the conversation about woolly creatures at an end, Algernon led Mr. Marshall to the library. A few embers glowed in the fireplace, and Algernon added a few blocks from the woodbin. He sat down facing his guest, noting the man's stiff, reserved manner.

Mr. Marshall cleared his throat. "I believe, Sir, you are acquainted with Ian Marshall, my father's other son."

"According to my understanding of family relationships, one's father's other son is a brother." Algernon spoke sharply, rather expecting to affront him, but instead, Marshall's proud demeanor faded.

"True, Ian is my brother. I have thought about him a great deal since my son…." He broke off, and Algernon remembered Ian saying his brother's only child had died. At the time, Algernon had cheerfully observed the death made Ian the heir apparent to Oakleigh. Facing the bereaved father, he felt deep compassion.

"Three days ago, I received a letter from Mr. Worthington of Hamstone. As I think you know, he claims—" he hesitated *"my brother* stole a cross from the church. He said it was worth at least five hundred pounds."

"Indeed, five hundred pounds, is it?" Algernon said, somehow not surprised. The squire of Oakleigh was a bigger fish than the owner of Longbourn, and the cross had become five times as valuable. No wonder Worthington had delayed accepting Algernon's offer. He hoped something more rewarding would land in his net.

Algernon retrieved Worthington's letter from a desk drawer. "Are you willing to pay Mr. Worthington five hundred pounds?"

"Yesterday, I went to see Mr. Worthington," Marshall said. "I told him I would pay the money to protect the family name, but...."

"Please continue."

"I must say I was not entirely impressed with him."

"Not impressed with Mr. Worthington?" Algernon was all amazement.

"It may be impolitic to say this, but I detected an aura of insincerity about him."

It was better than nothing. Still, if an aura was all Mr. Marshall detected, his perception was not quite breathtaking. "Mr. Marshall, I am certain he is lying about your brother. He has intimidated the maid and forced her to lie, too."

"Ian told me you believe he is innocent."

"You talked to him?" Algernon asked, surprised. "I saw him several days ago, and he never mentioned—"

"I saw Mr. Worthington yesterday. Then I went to the jail." Mr. Marshall's nose wrinkled at the memory "Ian said you offered to pay Worthington."

"He refused to allow it."

"He does not want me to pay. I must say that after seeing the jail, his attitude impresses me. I understand he was parson of your church."

Algernon explained he had first invited Ian to conduct the funeral service for the former parson. "Your brother was a curate under Mr. Worthington. His salary was a disgrace for the son of a squire." He stared at Marshall.

Marshall caught the look. "The Marshall family has, shall we say, reservations about Ian."

"So I concluded," Algernon said.

Marshall sat silent for a moment, then said, "We, certainly *I*, should have treated him better."

"He never complained about his treatment. To the contrary, he said he wished you and he could have been friends."

"Ian said he wished we could have been friends?" Marshall asked, his expression pensive.

"While in this room."

"Mr. Bennet, you like my brother."

"He is a fine young man."

There was a long silence. It was up to Marshall to break it. "The family did not regard Ian, because of his mother's lack of proper family and consequence. However, today he behaved with dignity despite those deplorable conditions. He...is a fine young man." Marshall repeated Algernon's words slowly, as if testing his belief in them.

Algernon did not know whether it was a desire to improve Mr. Marshall's opinion of his brother or delicious malice, but he said, "Perhaps, I should not mention this, but there is someone else who thinks highly of him."

He waited. Mr. Marshall was not cooperative enough to inquire. He had to proceed without being coaxed. "Mr. Darcy has a sister. She may be too young for a serious attachment. However, she and your brother...." He broke off at what he deemed the right place.

"Mr. Darcy's sister and my brother may have an attachment?" The pleasure in his voice suggested Ian's humble maternity would be more than offset by the pride inherent in a Marshall forming an alliance with the Darcys.

Deciding it was malice, Algernon continued: "Even without the current situation, there would be no point in talking about it. Miss Darcy is an heiress, thirty thousand pounds, I understand. Her guardians would surely disapprove of a relationship with a poor parson."

Mr. Marshall resumed his more imposing demeanor. "My brother is heir apparent to Oakleigh. When his name is cleared, no one, not even Mr. Darcy, could object to him as a suitor for a gentlewoman."

Algernon was pleased his father's other son had suddenly been promoted to a brother whose merit could be defended.

"I will talk to Mr. Darcy and assure him Mr. Worthington is mistaken. If Ian and Mr. Darcy's sister are attached—"

"Do not mention it!" Algernon said sharply. The young man was in jail; this was not the moment to tell Darcy about his sister's regard for him.

"I must get Ian out of that horrible place. I will insist he let me pay the five hundred pounds and—"

"Five hundred?" Algernon handed Mr. Marshall Worthington's letter.

Mr. Marshall read it, then crushed it in his hand, just as his brother had. "He asked you for one hundred. In his letter to me he said five hundred. " Marshall sputtered. "The man is definitely lying."

Abruptly, Marshall began to flatten the letter. "We must confront him with this letter, and the letter he sent me. Together, they prove he is lying about the value of the cross. If he realizes we can convince the court he is lying, he will have to withdraw his complaint."

"With both letters, we will still have the maid to contend with," Algernon said, going to the sideboard. He opened a bottle of brandy, apricot brandy. He filled two snifters and handed one to his guest. "I have a better idea."

Chapter 25

Suddenly, there was a din of feminine voices, and Algernon said, "Mr. Marshall, I think my daughters and house guest have returned." He had just finished laying out his plan, and Mr. Marshall was mulling it over:

"How can you be certain it will work?"

Algernon poured his guest more brandy. "I can hardly be certain, but it is worth trying."

Mr. Marshall looked apprehensive. "It would mean publicizing my brother's predicament."

"I am afraid the entire situation is already well-reported in every parish between here and Hamstone, and probably in every neighboring county." Algernon swirled his brandy. "A fast horse cannot keep up with gossip."

Marshall set his snifter on the side table. "Mr. Bennet, you impress me as a man of keen insight and good judgment. I will agree to what you have in mind."

Algernon realized Mr. Marshall was far more discerning than a first impression conveyed. "You were willing to pay Mr. Worthington five hundred pounds. May I count on you for that amount?"

"I would far rather pay to clear Ian's name honorably than pay money to Mr. Worthington."

They stood up and struck hands. They had an agreement. Algernon would not really have minded losing a chess game to Darcy, but now he was principal player in a game he had to win.

They returned to the drawing room where Algernon expected to find three ladies. Instead, he found five. Miss Darcy had arrived, accompanied by Mrs. Annesley, who traveled as her chaperon. When Algernon presented Mr. Marshall, Miss Darcy stood close to Elizabeth, her manner shy in a way easily mistaken for aloofness.

On hearing Miss Darcy's name, Mr. Marshall's manner changed. Accepting Georgiana's hand, he held it gently and almost smiled.

"Mr. Marshall," she said, sounding impressed. "You must be related." Her shyness dropped away in a display of delight.

"Miss Darcy, I am his brother," Marshall said, his smile broadening

"Whose brother?" Darcy questioned.

"Mr. Ian Marshall," Georgiana said, eagerly. "I met him when I visited here before." Her expression changed and, catching herself, she cast a furtive eye at Elizabeth.

"I have not the pleasure of his acquaintance," Darcy said. "I look forward to meeting him."

Not wanting to announce that, at the moment, any pleasure of the kind would have to take place in jail, Algernon quickly changed the subject, loudly welcoming Miss Darcy and Mrs. Annesley to Longbourn.

When he had suggested to Mr. Marshall that an attachment existed between his brother and Miss Darcy, his intention had been to drive home the point that Ian was acceptable in good society. He did not suspect that within minutes he would be introducing him to the lady. Now, seeing the inquisitive look on Darcy's face, he regretted his bit of mischief and was not disappointed when Mr. Marshall declined his invitation to stay to dinner. The less contact this Marshall had with Miss Darcy and her brother, the better.

At first, Algernon thought his mischief had been harmless, but after the company dispersed to their apartments to dress, he heard muffled crying, and then Georgiana Darcy's impassioned voice. "Mr. Bennet thinks he is innocent, and I am sure he would not steal. William, we must help him."

Puzzled, Algernon suddenly remembered that Darcy's mother was a Fitzwilliam, and that was his Christian name. The shortened *William* had to be leftover from childhood. In distress, she had used it.

"Georgiana, is that why you were so eager to visit Longbourn again? To see him?"

"When you meet him, you will—"

"I do not expect to meet someone who is in jail for theft."

Algernon could have closed his bedroom door but instead, stepped into the hallway. Miss Darcy ran passed him, oblivious to his presence, and made her way down the stairs. He heard a door close. She had taken refuge in *his* library.

Algernon could not fault himself for eavesdropping. He had played a role and had no way to make amends if uninformed.

"Darcy, if he is innocent, you should give him a chance. When Georgiana told me about him, I—"

"When she told you about him!" Darcy sounded incredulous. "Elizabeth, my sister wanted to come here to pursue an acquaintance with a man who is at best a poor clergyman—at worst, God knows—and you kept it from me?"

"I could not betray her confidence."

"Elizabeth, remember George Wickham."

Algernon was headed back to his room when he heard the name. He stopped, and what he heard next explained the bad blood between his sons-in-law. Georgiana Darcy had once been sufficiently en- amored by Wickham to contemplate an elopement. It sounded as if Darcy had learned of it just in time to save his sister who, Algernon reckoned, could have been little more than fifteen.

Ah, if only Wickham had married Miss Darcy and left the Bennet family alone! No, on second thought, Algernon realized it did not matter. With- out Wickham to run away with, Lydia would have attached herself to some other daring rascal in an irresistible red coat.

He could not catch all of Elizabeth's words, but heard enough to realize she was insisting that if Marshall's imprisonment was unjust, it should not be held against him.

Voices rose and fell. The Darcys were arguing. Algernon was certain they would argue only about something serious—such as his sister's welfare— and realized he might be overhearing their first heated dispute. He regretted it for Elizabeth's sake. He would have preferred to think she was in a perfect marriage, yet surely they were as entitled as any other couple to the acrimony of matrimony.

"My dearest, your father is not the best judge of people. Yesterday, you yourself said he does not realize what is going on here. I still think you should alert him to it."

"Usually he *is* a very good judge. What you are thinking of is a totally different matter. I cannot—I will not—presume to inform him."

Algernon was baffled. Nothing was going on at Longbourn. He had no idea what Darcy could mean.

Chapter 26

Pushing open the door to the library, Algernon peeked inside. He wanted his room but had no desire to encounter a weeping female. Fortunately, Miss Darcy had left. The room was his and, settling himself at his desk, he took a fresh sheet from his sketchpad.

Although his artwork was usually for his eyes only, he hoped the effort he had in mind would be widely seen. He began by drawing a cross. Perhaps it did not resemble the missing cross, but it was the idea that mattered. Lettering was not his forte. He was struggling to get it right when Hill knocked.

"Sir, I am sorry to interrupt you, but there is something…"

"What, Hill?"

"I have to apologize for Sarah. She is down in the kitchen crying. She is sorry—and so am I—for the damage she did the young lady. She had no idea the trouble she was causing."

He looked up. "What damage are you talking about?"

"She upset the young lady by telling her about poor Mr. Marshall. When the lady asked after him, Sarah knew no better than to tell her he was in jail. The lady insisted on knowing why. When Sarah told her all of it—"

"All of it?" Algernon questioned.

"Indeed, Sir. Sarah told her he was accused of stealing a priceless gold cross, the household silver, and many pounds in tithes. The young lady broke into tears." Hill looked close to tears herself.

Miraculously, rumor had transformed the cross into gold, then added generous tithes and the household silver. Algernon expected, at the next telling, the poor man would be accused of making off with the church steeple.

"Please tell Sarah to dry her tears. Miss Darcy asked about Mr. Marshall. If Sarah had not told her, she would have found out elsewhere."

Miss Darcy had sought information and learned of Ian Marshall's imprisonment on her own. The unlikely romance Algernon suggested to Alexander Marshall had not set the stage for the uproar he heard. He felt relieved but did not look forward to taking his place at the head of the dinner table. If

Miss Darcy appeared at all, she was apt to be viewing the world through red-eyes. After an argument with her husband, even his dear Elizabeth was unlikely to be a source of cheer.

When they assembled, Miss Darcy was missing. Algernon offered his arm to Miss Pepper, choosing a person neutral to the day's events. They would lead the way. Darcy offered his arm to his wife, but Elizabeth invited Mary to take her place. Elizabeth was pairing with Mrs. Annesley when Miss Darcy joined them.

Algernon was surprised to see her, even more surprised to observe her manner. Usually demure, now she walked with her head tilted up. Her chin may have quivered, but her expression was defiant.

Through the soup course, the only conversation was between Miss Pepper and Mrs. Annesley with an occasional astute contribution from Mary. Darcy seemed unable to keep his eyes off his wife. If they were at war, he was hoisting the flag of surrender.

As the butler gathered the soup bowls, Miss Darcy cleared her throat. "Mr. Bennet," she began, speaking in a clear voice, "I was told Mr. Ian Marshall is incarcerated and accused of theft. My dear sister Elizabeth told me that you—"

"Not now, Georgiana!"

For a moment, Georgiana looked dismayed but, ignoring her brother, she tilted her head higher and seemed to gather courage. She took a deep breath. "Mr. Bennet, is it true you believe Mr. Marshall is innocent?"

"Georgiana! I explained that whether he is innocent or guilty does not matters. The point is—"

Algernon held up his hand. "Mr. Darcy, I have to disagree with you. To answer your sister's question, yes, I believe Ian Marshall is innocent and it does matter."

Algernon was a bit amazed with himself for contradicting Darcy, especially in the presence of his wife and sister. The man's impressive manner usually assured Algernon's compliance, but not this time. He believed in Ian and had to assert himself. "I think Mr. Worthington is a liar who accused Mr. Marshall to punish him for leaving his employ and to extort money. I intend to do everything I can to expose the truth."

"Sir," Darcy said, his expression softening, "your opinion of him does him credit."

"Theft is a serious crime, deserving of unpleasant consequences to the thief. Therefore, every precaution should be taken to assure an innocent person is not wrongfully convicted. If an accused person is found to be innocent, we must restore his good name."

"Mary, you are quite right, and I am certain we all hope the truth will come out," Miss Pepper said.

Without pausing, she continued: "I am instructed to convey a most agreeable message to all of you." She smiled expectantly, but no one paid her the courtesy of inquiring.

Finally, Algernon spoke up, "Miss Pepper, as you can see, we all eagerly anticipate your news."

"When we were in Meryton this morning, I saw Mrs. Long. She told me that we would receive an invitation to a ball they are giving on Friday. I think a ball will be a delightful way to end the holiday season."

"Indeed!" Algernon said, feeling more interest than he usually did at news of a ball. "Lizzy, I am sure you will want to attend."

Her husband had her attention, and she seemed not to hear. Darcy's disapproving expression was gone. Gazing at his wife, he looked loving. She looked forgiving. With good luck, they would have other quarrels, but today's ice was melting.

Later, Algernon locked himself in the library and rearranged the furniture. The desk was too heavy and had to remain in place. The chairs and side tables he pushed against the wall, clearing the center of the room.

With weightier concerns on his mind, he had not had time to dwell on the absurdity of Mr. Collins and his in-laws thinking he might marry again and father a son.

I caution you on both practical and moral grounds.

Those had been Mr. Collins's words. Algernon had ample experience being impractical, but he was never immoral. Was he ever cruel? Considering what would be a suitable punishment for them, he decided a little cruelty might be called for.

Approaching a chair, he smiled charmingly and positioned his left arm behind his back, then bowed low, sweeping his right arm in a wide arc. Standing up, he reached and gently grasped the air. He nodded and smiled in all directions as he moved with light steps to the middle of the floor. Humming a melody for the quadrille, he paused, bowed again, and began to dance. Visualizing himself in mind's eye, he was captivated.

Chapter 27

Algernon looked over the previous day's work. He had drawn a cross and beneath it, he had inked an announcement in thick letters. It was only a sign, not a work of art, but he decided it was too plain.

On a second sign, in addition to the cross, he drew a finely detailed church in a lower corner. He drew larger crosses and put leaves in the borders of the next two signs, and on the fifth sign he enjoyed scrolling a graceful, stemmed lily across the top.

The message was always the same:

£200 Reward

For information that aids recovery of an ebony and silver cross missing from Hamstone church. An innocent man is charged with its theft.

> *Algernon Bennet, Esquire*
> *Longbourn, Hertfordshire*

He gladly put his name under the assertion that Ian Marshall was innocent. When Ian was cleared, everyone would know his faith in his young parson never wavered.

Deciding how much to offer for a reward had been difficult. At first, Algernon had thought five hundred pounds, the sum Alexander Marshall had agreed to pay to benefit his recently acknowledged brother. Then he had reconsidered. To anyone with good information, two hundred pounds was likely to be a great deal of money. Although extravagance might be gratifying at someone else's expense, he decided two hundred pounds was as likely as five to bring results.

He spread the signs over his desk. The one with the lily was the best and should go to the post in Meryton in case word got out identifying it as his work. The second best should be displayed in the window of a Meryton shop. The last three were for display at the post and in busy shops in Hamstone.

The signs were finished, but there was something else he had to do. When the ink on the last sign was drying, he penned a brief note to Mr. Allen inviting him to conduct Sunday services again. It pleased Algernon to have thought of it before Miss Pepper felt obliged to remind him.

He rang for the butler and told him to send Miss Pepper and Mary. Miss Pepper arrived in moments, and he casually pointed to the signs. " If you would be so kind, I would like you and Mary to display them at the post offices in Hamstone and Meryton, and in prominent shops."

Miss Pepper took her time looking at the signs. "I will be happy to take them," she said, "and I know Mary will want to help, too." She hesitated. "Mr. Bennet, do you think they will bring results?"

When talking to Alexander Marshall, Algernon had acted more confident than he felt. Now he said, "I do not know, but I think—I hope—they will."

"What will we do if no one comes forward?"

That question was heavy on Algernon's mind. "I will try to find a way to talk to the maid who claims she saw Mr. Marshall steal the cross," he said, his voice weary. "If her conscience is bothering her, she may admit Worthington forced her to lie."

"Sir, she should be told that if the cross is found in a way that proves Mr. Marshall did not take it, her false testimony could put *her* in prison."

This leverage had not occurred to Algernon, and Miss Pepper was right. Getting the maid to recant might prove more effective than a few signs, and so might the two letters showing Mr. Worthington's different assessments of the value of the cross.

"The sign with the lily is the best work," Miss Pepper said. "I think it should be hung in the post office in Meryton."

He held back a smile at her appreciation of his finer work. "You may decide which goes where."

On impulse, he picked up the note he had just penned and waved it at her. "I am inviting Mr. Allen to conduct services again."

"Have you had time to inspect the parsonage since Mrs. Hendrick moved out?"

"Not yet," he said, not mentioning that the idea had never occurred to him.

"Mary and I happened to pass it on our walk. The door was unlatched, and we checked inside. Dear Mrs. Hendrick left several items of furniture. A few additions would make it quite comfortable. " She smiled. "I hope you will not think us presumptuous for making a little list of the repairs you will want to have attended to while it is vacant."

Before he could frame a suitable retort to her "little list of repairs," Mary appeared.

"Mary, your father made these excellent signs." She held one up for Mary's inspection. "If you are willing, we will take them for display in Meryton and Hamstone."

"I will gladly participate in a noble effort to free a man from unjust confinement."

Pausing, Mary seemed struck by a happy idea. "I will ask Miss Darcy to accompany us." Her voice dropped to a confidential whisper. "I believe she likes Mr. Marshall."

Algernon placed an affectionate hand on her shoulder. "My dear Mary, your perception astounds me," he said, always amused by people who were pleased with themselves for cleverly detecting the obvious.

"I do not think Mr. Darcy would want his sister to go with us on *this* errand," Miss Pepper said.

Algernon thought so, too, but was not about to agree with everything the woman said. "Mary, you may invite her if you wish. Whether or not she goes should be her decision."

"I have been neglecting my studies and hope to finish this book tomorrow," Mary said, holding up her ever-present book. "But I will spare time to go to Meryton tomorrow, and on Friday, we can go to Hamstone."

"No," Algernon said. "The trip to Hamstone will take most of the day. You need to go tomorrow. On Friday, you can go to Meryton early and get back in time for our commitment."

"Papa, what commitment do you mean?"

He looked at her askance. "My dear Mary, how could you forget? We are all engaged to attend the ball at the Longs."

The next morning, he ordered the carriage. Mrs. Annesley had returned to Derbyshire, and he assigned Mr. Stanley to accompany three ladies, to Hamstone. When told why Mary and Miss Pepper were going, Miss Darcy had been determined to accompany them.

"Mr. Bennet," she said as he walked them all to the carriage, "it was so good of you to make the signs. I am sure Mr. Marshall will be grateful. He told me you were the best friend he ever had."

The best friend he ever had. The words stung. He had promised to help Ian get out of jail, and all he had come up with was a few signs that, at heart, he admitted were unlikely to bring results.

The ladies were gone most of the day. On their return, Miss Pepper assured him the signs were well displayed. "The moment we hung the sign in the butcher's window, a crowd gathered to read it. People who do not see it themselves are certain to hear about it."

Algernon wondered how dear Mr. Worthington would react if news of the signs reached him.

Chapter 28

Elizabeth looked skeptical when Algernon told her he planned to attend the ball at the Longs. "I think it will be a very pleasant occasion for all of us," he said at breakfast.

"Father, you are not serious. When mother was here, you hated escorting us to social events."

"Elizabeth, I owe it to society to share in the merry making of the season."

His favorite daughter laughed. "You, claiming to feel obliged to attend a ball! You are not serious."

"Elizabeth, I am not teasing. I am going."

"Sir, you need not attend on our account. Elizabeth and I would gladly forego the ball in favor of your company here. Do not think—"

"Darcy, I am going, and I hope Elizabeth and you will accompany me."

Algernon was glad the other ladies were not yet downstairs because Darcy was still unaware of the purpose for their trip to Hamstone. "An errand of mine," is the only explanation he had given when Darcy had asked, and the less mention of it the better. Darcy would hardly rejoice to find out his sister had been in public, hanging signs to help free a man from prison.

It was midday when the three ladies set out to take the last two signs to Meryton. Watching the carriage leave, Algernon was glad the signs would advertise his belief in Ian's innocence even if unlikely to solicit information to clear him. It hurt to admit the signs in Hamstone were almost as hopeless. If Worthington still had the cross—and Algernon suspected he did—no one could know; no one would be able to help.

It was time to put Ian out of mind, at least for one evening. Dressing for the ball, Algernon took more than usual care with his appearance and even considered sending for powder to powder his hair, something he had never done. After a brief reflection, he decided against it. His hair was thick. In the candle glow of a ballroom, the auburn shade would look a dark brown. That would have to be handsome enough.

Although he had rarely managed to respect his wife in life, he tried to show her proper respect in death by always wearing black ribbons when he left Longbourn—but a black ribbon would be inappropriate at a ball. He pondered, then folded the circle of black satin and tucked it into his pocket, content in the knowledge he would not be leaving it home. He also pocketed fine, white gloves, a long-ago birthday gift from Jane, which he had never worn.

When the party assembled, Algernon was struck with Georgiana Darcy's appearance. She looked quite lovely; her hair adorned with jeweled feathers, the pink of her dress the color of apple blossoms. "Miss Darcy," he said, "may I tell you how nice you look this evening?"

"Thank you, Mr. Bennet," she said, giving him a graceful curtsey.

Her manner, more than her attire, gave her a different presence. Although she had been honored at not one, but two, coming-out balls—the first at Pemberley, the second, a reportedly lavish affair at Rosings, her aunt's estate—she had still seemed girlish. Now her confident air said she had decided to be grown up.

Darcy's carriage was large enough to accommodate all six in the party, but Algernon insisted on traveling in his own barouche. When he arrived at the Longs, several carriages were ahead of his. He waited, and when the footman opened the door and lowered the stair, he stepped down eagerly.

Algernon moved quickly through the receiving line, then found himself a corner deep in shadows. When accompanying his wife and daughters to parties, he had often sought such a corner, more entertained as an observer than as a participant. Tonight, it was simply habit.

The corner was near the musicians, and he noted the ensemble consisted of two violins, a bass violin, a flute, harp, and clarinet. The musicians were not local, and their presence marked this as an elegant ball. A more humble affair would usually boast only a local violinist or two, perhaps accompanied by someone at the pianoforte.

Elizabeth and Darcy came toward him, making their way past several people. "Father, I knew I would find you off by yourself," she said, taking his arm. "Come, they are serving the syllabub now."

"Syllabub? My dear, that is a concoction for ladies."

"I will get yours with brandy instead of sherry, and with less whipped cream."

"No syllabub for me," he said, freeing his arm. "Now you must excuse me." Walking away, he put on the white gloves, delighted to have his Lizzy standing witness.

"Sir William, Lady Lucas," Algernon said after going out of his way to get their attention, "what a splendid evening." Before they could answer, he made his way to where Mary and Miss Pepper were seated.

Standing in front of Miss Pepper, he smiled charmingly, then positioned his left arm behind his back and bowed low, sweeping his right arm in a wide arc, just as he had practiced. "Miss Pepper, will you honor me with the first two dances?"

Instantly on her feet, she extended her hand.

"Papa! You cannot really...I mean, are you going to dance?"

"Mary, you may watch and see."

Nodding and smiling in all directions, Algernon led his partner to the floor where they took places in the set. The music played. The ladies curtsied; the gentlemen bowed, and the dance began. Holding Miss Pepper's hand, he led her down the line.

He had the attention of the room, exactly as he had wished; however, dancing proved more difficult at a ball than in his library. One of her feet managed to get beneath his. She continued to smile, so he hoped she had not noticed.

Her smile was so radiant, he was confident she understood. A perceptive woman, she realized the Lucases and Mr. Collins anxiously suspected them of matrimonial intent, and they were being punished for such impudence.

One of her feet got beneath his again. "Sorry, my dear," he whispered.

When the dance ended, he led his partner to her chair and withdrew. He was ready to join Elizabeth and Darcy, but they were joining the next dance.

Deliberately strolling past Sir William and his lady, he noticed with delight how blanched she looked. Although anyone that white could not be hot, her husband was busy fanning her. Algernon had no fears for her health, confident only his dancing had set her wrong.

He was not the evening's oldest dancer. Several men his age and older were taking to the floor. Mr. Caulfield, whom Algernon knew had celebrated his twentieth birthday before he managed his first, was beaming and lightfooting it down the line. His dancing offered the assembly no novelty. He always danced when he could secure a partner, but his approach was apt to send the ladies scattering. Algernon's dancing was different. Even neighbors of many years had never seen him dance. He was surrounded by stares and murmurs.

Miss Darcy was going down the dance. As she passed near him, Algernon heard a whispered, "Mr. Bennet." He caught her meaningful smile and was surprised by a moment of wordless communication between them. She could not express herself at Longbourn, but she trusted him to help Ian.

He accepted a glass of sherry from a tray and was retreating to his corner when he saw Mr. Allen lead Miss Pepper to the dance. He realized, more now than when he had danced with her, that Miss Darcy was not the only lady whose appearance was much improved. Miss Pepper actually looked pretty, and she carried herself well.

He was not entirely pleased to see her dance with someone else. Sir William and his lady might think it diluted the fear of impending matrimony her dance with him was meant to excite. To secure his point, he engaged Miss Pepper for the next two dances and the two after that.

He quite enjoyed himself and regretted that Miss Pepper's feet wandered under his more times than once. She never lost her smile, although she did seem to limp a bit as he led her to the supper table. Sir William and Lady Lucas were already seated and stared at them with ill-disguised horror. He gave Miss Pepper a conspiratorial wink, and her grasp on his arm tightened.

At dinner, Algernon caught Elizabeth's attention and was disappointed when she did not return his telling look. He had no doubt she understood what he was up to, and he suspected she was wasting sympathy on the suffering parents of her friend, Charlotte.

Miss Pepper was not the only sought-after lady in their party. Miss Darcy had every single man in attendance pleading for a dance with her. Mary, usually devoted to adorning the wall, was solicited and danced several times. Time passed so quickly, Algernon was surprised when the musicians packed their instruments.

Carriages were sent for, and Darcy was handing Miss Pepper into his when she drew back. "I must go and find my glove."

Several minutes passed, and now other carriages waited behind Darcy's. "Go," Algernon told him. "I do not think Miss Pepper will mind riding home with me,"

Darcy said, "Mr. Bennet, allow me to assure you, the lady will not mind."

Moments after their carriage left, Miss Pepper returned. "Please, forgive me," she said, holding up a glove. "It was tucked inside the other one, and I did not see it."

"Quite all right," Algernon said, handing her into his barouche.

"What a delightful evening," she said.

Algernon agreed, but a night of dancing was more fatiguing than he had expected. Resting his head on the back cushion, he enjoyed recalling the amazed stares of the Lucases and other neighbors. "Miss Pepper, we showed them, did we not?"

In the darkness he could hardly see her but thought she was smiling. "Indeed," she said softly, "we certainly did."

Chapter 29

In the moonlight, Algernon's beloved trees cast intricate shadows on snow that sparkled like a scattering of crystals. A lone, dark cloud drifted across a field of stars. Looking out his bedroom window, Algernon felt the tranquility of the scene and was at peace with the world—possibly even with the Lucases. He had enjoyed his revenge, and they had suffered enough. He resolved to pay an early visit and assure them a second marriage did not loom in his future.

He was about to close the drape when he caught a glimpse of something moving slowly along the lane. When he could make it out, he realized it was a dog sled. A figure wrapped in a blanket hunched behind the driver. Dawn was hours away, an unlikely time for anyone to have business at Longbourn. Algernon realized it had to be an emergency.

Perhaps, a relative of a servant had taken ill or died. He expected the cart to go around to the servants' door. Instead, it stopped at the main entrance. The driver helped the hunched figure climb out.

It was a woman, and a moment later she was pounding on the door. The butler and Hill would be sound asleep. Instead of trying to rouse someone, Algernon pulled on his robe, ignited a spindle from glowing wood in the fireplace, and relit his candle.

Going into the hall, he saw a figure approaching and, in the halo of her candle, he recognized Miss Pepper. Her hair flowed long and loose under a lacy nightcap, and a shawl draped around her shoulders.

"Mr. Bennet," she whispered, "perhaps I can help."

Without answering, he went downstairs and pressed his ear close to the thick door. "Who is it?"

"I am come to see the master." The words were accented by the chatter of teeth.

"Why do you want to see him?"

"I can tell no one but himself."

"I am the master," Algernon said, opening the door.

The woman stepped inside and, leaning her face close to his, asked anxiously, "You are Mr. Bennet? Mr. Algernon Bennet, squire of Longbourn?"

"I am. What business do you have with me at this hour?"

"I had to come now. I dare not risk what would happen if I came by daylight and he found me out."

"If *who* found you out?" Miss Pepper asked. She had followed Algernon downstairs and stood close behind him.

The woman took another look at Algernon, then gave Miss Pepper a nervous glance. "You must never tell. Please, I beg you both, never tell."

"There is nothing I can tell," Algernon said. "You have not told me anything—not even your name."

"I am Mrs. Jennings."

"Mrs. Jennings?" He had heard the name but could not place it.

"I am Mr. Worthington's housekeeper."

Miss Pepper clasped her hands. "Our signs! You are here, because you saw one of our signs!"

"Indeed, Ma'am, that is right. We saw a sign, a two hundred pound reward, it said. As soon as it was dark, my son hitched his dogs to the sled and we started out." She hesitated. "My son is outside. The cold is fierce."

Algernon opened the door. "He can come in."

"James!" she called.

Her son did not need a second summons and hurried to the house.

Miss Pepper told him to come with her. "The kitchen is warm and you can wait there while your mother talks to Mr. Bennet." The look she gave Algernon begged him not to let her miss anything.

He took Mrs. Jennings into the sitting room, pointed to a chair close to the fireplace, and stoked the embers to raise a feeble blaze. "Miss Pepper will be here in a moment. Then you can tell us both."

Miss Pepper joined them before he could finish.

Mrs. Jennings folded her hands in her lap, composing herself, then began: "He was on his way to the church, and—"

"Do you mean Mr. Worthington?" Algernon asked, pulling his chair close to hers.

"Yes, Sir. Mr. Worthington. He was on his way to the church. He is a round man, rounder every year I think, and walking does not agree with him. He was struggling to get on when I happened by. Coming back from the hen house, I was. He handed me an old shirt and said I must go to the church and fetch the silver and black cross. I had to wrap it all up in the shirt and bring it to his study."

Algernon tensed. "When was this?"

She looked thoughtful, then shook her head. "I am not good with dates."

"Do not bother about the date! Do you know if Ian Marshall was still Mr. Worthington's curate?" Algernon held his breath.

"It was some days after the poor young man left. I do remember that," she said proudly.

Miss Pepper stood at Algernon's side. At Mrs. Jennings's words, her hand clutched his shoulder. "Mr. Bennet, this proves Mr. Marshall could not have stolen the cross."

Algernon rested his hand over Miss Pepper's. "No one stole it. I think the man still has it."

"Aye, Sir, that is my thought in coming here."

"Mrs. Jennings, do you know where the cross is now?" Miss Pepper asked.

"Ma'am, all I can tell you is that when I brought it to him, his big strong box was open and on his desk."

"A maid told the magistrate she saw Mr. Marshall pack the cross in his valise. If the court believes her—"

Mrs. Jennings did not let him finish. "Sir, what poor Bridget said does not matter. Mr. Worthington frightened her so terrible, she sold every stick she owned to make passage back to Ireland. When I saw the fine young ladies posting notices saying Mr. Marshall was innocent and offering such a grand reward, I knew—"

"What!"

Algernon did not glance toward the doorway, too involved with Mrs. Jennings to deal with Darcy.

"Mr. Bennet, am I understanding this correctly? Yesterday, when my sister and the other ladies went to Hamstone, they posted a sign to assist a man imprisoned for theft? With your knowledge, my sister exposed herself in such a way?"

"So it would seem," Algernon said vaguely. "And they posted signs in Meryton."

"Sir, you are Elizabeth's father. I respect you," Darcy said in a tone more angry than respectful. "However, I must say I disapprove—very much disapprove—of what you allowed my sister to do."

"Mr. Darcy, we posted the signs because we know Ian Marshall is innocent. What Mrs. Jennings tells us confirms it." Miss Pepper spoke softly, a hardly necessary precaution. Almost the whole household was up.

Rising to her feet, Mrs. Jennings clasped her hands. "I beg you, do not let Mr. Worthington know I told. I do not want to lose my post unless...."

"If we can prove what you tell us, your reward will equal many years' wages," Algernon said.

"*My* reward!" Mrs. Jennings hands were still clasped. She looked prayerful.

Algernon never doubted the woman was telling the truth, but Mr. Worthington was a clergyman. His word against hers would carry more weight—perhaps not weight commensurate to his own—but enough to promote his credibility.

Darcy approached Mrs. Jennings. He was not in nightclothes but wore trousers and an unbuttoned shirt that hung loose. "What is your name?"

As Algernon introduced them, Mrs. Jennings curtsied. "The others will not tell Mr. Worthington. Please, Sir—"

Darcy held up his hand, silencing her. "Mrs. Jennings, I understand the cross was distinctive—that is, quite different than most."

"Yes, indeed, Sir. I never saw one the least like it, with the silver and wood and all."

Darcy nodded, seeming to have received the answer he expected. "Do you remember it?"

"Sir, I remember that cross, same as if I was looking at it this minute."

"Mr. Bennet, Elizabeth told me you are quite an accomplished artist."

"Accomplished? No, indeed not. I draw. I paint a bit, that is all." Algernon said, uneasy at having his art mentioned.

"Your work is excellent," Miss Pepper said.

"Let us see how excellent it is. Mr. Bennet, I want you to draw the cross exactly the way Mrs. Jennings describes it."

"In the morning, I can try but—"

"It is morning now," Darcy said.

Algernon shrugged. "I will try it in the library, and I will need more candles."

Miss Pepper led the way and, in the library, lit working candles and arranged them to best light his desk. Algernon laid out paper, poised his pen, and awaited Mrs. Jennings's description. She held up her hands showing the size of the cross, then she gave details as she remembered them.

"It was like it had two layers. The bottom layer was black, shiny wood. The silver on top was smaller so wood edges showed around it about this much." She held up a thumb and forefinger. "The sides of the wood were cut straight. The silver— how can I say it? The sides of the silver were like this." She moved her hand in a soft arc. "A little star was engraved at the top of the silver where letters usually are."

The only sound was Algernon's pen on the paper as he drew and shaded. At first, he felt uneasy having people watch him work; then he forgot his audience, forgot he was tired, and lost himself in the task. The crosses he had drawn for the signs had been his own design. Now he worked as instructed.

"Oh, Sir," Mrs. Jennings said when Algernon finished. "It looks just like it."

"Elizabeth told me the cross was reported to be very unusual, and this is better than I had hoped," Darcy said, studying the drawing, He waited until the ink was dry, then rolled up the drawing and crushed it a little. Algernon was too weary—and too proud—to plead for an explanation.

"Mr. Bennet," Mrs. Jennings said anxiously, "I dare not have Mr. Worthington suspect me. My son and I must start for home. T'is a long way, and we will be hours on the road."

Algernon insisted that she and her son stay and have breakfast. They would be conveyed home, dogs and sled, too, in his hay wagon with his steward driving a two-horse team.

Unrolling the drawing, Darcy gave it another look. "Miss Pepper is correct," he said smiling. "Your work is excellent. When we are dressed and breakfasted, we must take this to Hamstone."

Algernon raised his eyebrows. "Indeed!" He had wanted to sound affronted at being issued orders. Instead, his voice broke on a yawn.

Chapter 30

D espite not touching his bed until almost dawn, Algernon arose earlier than usual. The brevity of sleep could not daunt his spirits. He now had confirmation that his suspicions were correct. Mr. Worthington still had the cross. He had to prove it and keep his promise to get Ian Marshall out of that wretched jail.

When the family gathered for breakfast, only Mary was unaware of the early morning excitement, and it was not mentioned. Algernon had promised Mrs. Jennings secrecy, and secrecy would be blown away if servants overheard such delicious news.

The only allusion occurred when Darcy ordered his carriage. "Yours might be recognized. We will take mine," he told Algernon.

Darcy had been angry when he realized his sister had publicly helped display signs to help an imprisoned man, yet he obviously had a plan of his own. As soon as they were in the carriage, Algernon expected an explanation.

Darcy began with, "Sir, am I right in thinking you believe Mr. Worthington still has the cross?"

"I am convinced of it."

"Elizabeth told me you took him to be a greedy man."

"Greedy and unscrupulous,"

"That is what we must count on," Darcy said

Algernon leaned toward him, expectant, but Darcy settled himself and looked out the window.

Nearing Hamstone, they caught up to the hay wagon. Mr. Jennings and her son were on the back, nestled under blankets from the stable. The sled was tied to the wagon, and three, very likely perplexed dogs crowded on the seat. Algernon gave a hearty wave as the carriage sped passed.

Darcy rapped for the coachman. "In Hamstone, you must find the magistrate's office," he said when the driver slid open the partition.

"Darcy, I can direct the coachman, but we cannot tell the magistrate what Mrs. Jennings said. Without proof, all we would accomplish is getting her discharged."

"We do not tell the magistrate anything," Darcy said. "We will simply ask him to accompany us when we pay Mr. Worthington a call."

His curiosity gnawed, but Algernon would not plead for an explanation. He shifted in his seat. His drawing of the cross had to play a part in his son-in-law's plan, but what, he agonized, was the plan?

Darcy entered the magistrate's office alone and returned accompanied by a spindly, wispy-haired man, yet to reach his middle years. "Mr. Faraday is assistant magistrate," Darcy said.

"Mr. Darcy," Mr. Faraday began, taking a seat facing Algernon, "your carriage is grand and this seat is wonderfully comfortable. Three years ago, I rode in a barouche. The interior was very nice, but not as fine as this." He ran his hand over the back of the seat, "I have never seen a better."

"Mr. Faraday," Darcy said, "you must pay close attention." He slipped his arms out of his coat and unbuttoned his shirt.

Although startled, Algernon was determined not to ask questions. If Darcy wanted to be mysterious, let him have his pleasure.

"As you see, I carry nothing but my money belt." Darcy handed Mr. Faraday his coat. "Do you agree there is nothing hidden in my coat?"

Looking bewildered, Mr. Faraday felt the coat. "Nothing is hidden," he said.

Darcy readjusted his clothes, and the driver was directed to Mr. Worthington's home. "I will see him alone," Darcy said. Before leaving the carriage, he tapped Algernon's knee with the rolled-up drawing. "Mr. Bennet, wish us luck."

"That I do," Algernon said, an idea starting to dawn.

Mr. Faraday's jabbering did little to shorten the wait: "This red upholstery is what I would want if I had a fine carriage. Not that I ever shall. My eldest brother has a gig. He was kind enough to loan it to me twice—once for a Sunday excursion and once to go to a burial. His horse is quite a nag. Old Maggie is reliable though and...."

Algernon looked at his watch for a second time and tried to ignore the incessant flow of words.

When Darcy returned, his face was inscrutable, neither cheerful nor dejected. He resumed his seat, sat silent for a moment, and then reached under his coat. He removed a cross, a silver cross mounted on an ebony base, and handed it to Mr. Faraday. "I believe this is the cross Mr. Worthington claimed Mr. Ian Marshall stole." He looked at Algernon. "I could not tell you what I was going to attempt, because I did not want you disappointed if it failed."

Algernon gave a nonchalant toss of his hand. "I understood when you wanted the drawing. I daresay you told Worthington it was a cross that belonged to your family, or some such story. You had been told Hamstone parish had a similar one, and you wanted to buy it. How much did you pay?"

Darcy started to laugh. "Six hundred pounds. Forgive me. I thought you were agitated, because I could not explain."

Algernon raised his eyebrows. "I am not often taken unawares."

Darcy looked at him. "Miss Pepper is also quite clever," he said.

Mr. Faraday bumped into the conversation. "If Mr. Worthington had the cross in his possession, why did he charge his curate with stealing it?"

"Let us ask him now. Mr. Bennet, would you like to accompany us?"

"You dare not go without me!"

The three men approached Mr. Worthington's door, and Algernon carried the cross.

"Elizabeth will be delighted when I tell her you always knew what I had in mind."

"She will hardly be surprised," Algernon said, pleased. "I take it my little sketch convinced him."

"I crumpled it so it would not look fresh, and I told Mr. Worthington it was a drawing of a cross in an old family portrait. I said I had heard Hamstone church had a cross just like it that I might want to buy. He was shaking his head until I mentioned six hundred pounds."

"How did you decide on that amount?"

"I needed to entice him, and it was all the travel money I had with me." A smile played the corner of

Darcy's mouth. "He demanded to see the money, and I counted it out on his desk. He stared at it, then went and got the cross."

Darcy's expression turned somber. "I knew if my deception worked, it would prove Mr. Marshall was innocent, but lying is absolutely against my principles. I abhor deception of any kind and always tell the truth."

Algernon patted his son-in-law's shoulder. "Do not be ashamed of your veracity. When the situation required, you overcame it."

A maid opened the door and led them to the study. Algernon could hardly wait. He was more than ready to encounter Robert Worthington.

The man appeared, dabbing his mouth with a napkin. He took a step backward, an expression of horror enveloping his face when he saw the recent purchaser of the cross accompanied by Algernon and the magistrate's assistant.

"My dear friend," Algernon said, beaming and extending his hand. "What a pleasure to see you." He pumped Worthington's hand with the enthusiasm shown to him on earlier visits.

"Mr. Bennet," Worthington's voice sounded more like a groan.

"We have an interesting situation," Algernon said, taking charge. "Mr. Faraday knows Mr. Darcy did not carry a cross into your home, yet he carried one out. You have just sold my son-in-law the cross you put Ian Marshall in jail for stealing. May we have your explanation?"

Worthington's lips moved in silence. Finally, he croaked, "A mistake. Terrible. Just discovered I still had…would have reported I found it. Tomorrow—no, today—I would have reported it. "

The relief Algernon felt knowing Ian would be freed did not offset his anger. Fury raged until he remembered that, in this room, the man trembling before him had insisted he could trust his life in Mrs. Jennings's hands. Surely, he had little suspected his life and credibility would one day be in her hands, and she would be eager to sell.

Instead of telling Worthington how contemptible he was, Algernon smiled, "Mr. Worthington, perhaps you would like to return Mr. Darcy's six hundred pounds."

Fumbling, Worthington opened a desk drawer, retrieved the stack of bank notes, and handed them to Darcy. His hand shook badly, either from shame or from grief at parting with his new wealth. When he reached to take the cross, Algernon allowed him to touch it and then pulled it out of his grasp.

"I think not. This goes to the magistrate."

Mr. Faraday contributed his bit of brilliance. "If Mr. Marshall did not steal the cross, he is mistakenly imprisoned."

"Indeed! I think Mr. Worthington would like to go to your office and withdraw the charge. Then he can accompany us to the jail to seek Mr. Marshall's release."

"No! I will send a statement. I will inform the magistrate that I blundered—that I made a terrible mistake—-but I will not go to the jail."

"Mr. Worthington, you will go to the magistrate with us now and then to the jail." Algernon's voice was very soft and absolutely to be obeyed.

Slumping, Worthington put his hand against the wall for support. "I will get my coat."

At the magistrate's office, Algernon watched as Worthington put his signature to papers dropping charges against Ian. He was not allowed to say simply that he had been mistaken. The details of his transaction with Darcy were included in a public statement.

Robert Worthington had come in his gig and begged to be allowed to return home. "You have Marshall's release papers. You do not need me."

Algernon stared at him. "Sir, you are going to explain yourself to Mr. Marshall."

A place in Darcy's carriage was not offered him and, lunging and struggling, Mr. Worthington piled himself back into his gig. Although Darcy's team could have overtaken it, the gig was obliged to lead the way. There could be no turning back.

Algernon wondered if his acquaintance with Obediah Dopple would be renewed, but in the entry they were met with another jailer, equally surly but with a less memorable name. "Do you mean you will be taking one out of here?" he said, his already unfriendly face twisting into a snarl.

"Only one," Algernon told him brightly. "You may keep the rest."

Algernon and Darcy waited with Worthington while the jailer shuffled off, eventually returning with a prisoner. It was a second before Algernon realized the bearded, bedraggled man was Ian.

"What is happening?" he asked, looking from Worthington to Algernon.

"Mr. Worthington will explain," Algernon said.

"Mr. Marshall, I have—I mean, I found the cross. Believe me, I never meant, truly never meant, for this to happen, for you to go to jail. Never thought it would go this far. Sorry, so sorry." The room where they crowded was chilly and damp, but as he babbled, Worthington ran his handkerchief over his forehead.

"Do you mean this is over? I am free?"

"Yes, my friend," Algernon said.

Ian closed his eyes. A weary smile lit his face. "Thank God."

Darcy extended his hand. "Sir, I am Fitzwilliam Darcy. I am sorry you were imprisoned."

"Darcy? Then you are her brother," Ian blurted.

It was a joyful moment and Darcy smiled. "Mr. Marshall, that would depend on who *she* is."

On the long journey back to Longbourn, Algernon told Ian how Darcy had exposed Worthington. "You owe your freedom to him, though you could have been released sooner if you had allowed your brother to pay Mr. Worthington."

"Mr. Darcy, I am forever indebted to you—to both of you—for your kindness and trouble. I was afraid I would be in jail for months, but I have never stolen anything. I could never allow anyone to pay as if I had."

"Mr. Bennet's high regard for you persuaded me to try to help. I laud his judgment, because your determination to stand your ground took character."

Algernon leaned back, pleased with himself for encouraging his companions' good opinion of each other. He had no ulterior motives. Elizabeth was wrong. He was not trying to assist a romantic attachment. Absolutely not.

Chapter 31

Algernon took great pleasure in writing to Mr. Marshall and explaining the circumstances of his brother's release. He was folding the letter when Miss Pepper appeared.

"Mr. Bennet, it is wonderful that your fine artistic talent was put to such noble use. Because of you, Mr. Marshall is free."

"It was Mr. Darcy's plan. I had no idea what he was up to." He surprised himself by acknowledging it to her.

"Your signs brought Mrs. Jennings and your drawing fooled Mr. Worthington. Your drawings are so good, it makes me want to ask—" She stopped abruptly. "Forgive me. It would have been most impolitic for me to ask."

"You did not ask. Until you do, I can hardly know if I forgive you."

She lowered her eyes. "I have never had my likeness drawn."

"Well, then," he said briskly, "perhaps I should give it a try."

He franked his letter and sent it express, expecting an early response. It was forthcoming but not in the form of a letter. Several days later, Mr. Marshall arrived at Longbourn. He requested a private meeting with Ian, and Algernon surrendered his library. When the brothers finally emerged, it was obvious that, at long last, they were friends. The elder seemed genuinely proud of the younger whose lowborn mother was apparently no longer an impediment to fraternal affection.

Rearranging his memory, Algernon told Mr. Marshall his signs had promised a reward of three hundred pounds, and that was the amount Alexander Marshall paid Mrs. Jennings. Since Marshall had been willing to pay five hundred pounds to secure his brother's release, he was two hundred pounds ahead. If Mrs. Jennings received a hundred pounds more than she had expected, no one could complain. It delighted Algernon to contemplate her happiness and Worthington's discomfort when she left his employ, and he realized what she had done.

An exceptionally cheerful group gathered to go into dinner. Algernon asked Elizabeth and Darcy to lead the way; he invited Mr. Marshall to be so kind as to escort Mary. He offered his arm to Miss Pepper, and that left Ian Marshall and Miss Darcy. Algernon did not look behind him as they entered the dining hall, confident the arrangement met with their approval.

At dinner, Ian Marshall said he had decided not to bring charges against Mr. Worthington. "He wrote to my brother hoping to wrest money from him, and it brought about our friendship." He looked across the table at his brother who returned his smile. "I am grateful."

Ian explained that Worthington had a lifetime bequest of Hamstone church, which meant he would keep his position, but he had lost his reputation. In view of the public statements he had been forced to make, even the poorest curate would be afraid to work for him. He would have to get out and do his own work. Knowing his treachery, parishioners would be sparse with their tithes and, best of all, his wife would add her dissatisfaction to his problems. Algernon thought they were the most suitable punishments Worthington could receive.

The next morning, Mr. Marshall left for Oakleigh, but not until telling Algernon he was making a financial settlement on Ian, suitable for the son of a squire and the heir apparent to a great estate. "Mr. Bennet, I cannot express all my appreciation for what you have done for my brother and me. Ian's praise of you is well-deserved. I would be proud to call you a friend."

"If you are my friend, the honor is mine."

After Marshall left, the Darcys agreed to extend their visit for a week. Of course, Algernon disdained the foolish idea it had been his intent, but the week provided time for Ian and Georgiana to enjoy each other's company. Their pleasure was obvious, and the young woman whom Algernon had once thought not very pretty, now had a glow that made her beautiful.

When they had a chance encounter in the upstairs corridor, she startled Algernon by grasping his arm and stretching tall to kiss his cheek. "You are so good, so kind," she said. "Ian and I are forever grateful. I am proud your daughter is my sister." Flustered, Algernon could think of nothing to say and was relieved when she hurried off.

Later, Ian joined him for a walk. Despite a sharp wind, gloomy gray sky and dirty puddles of melting snow sloshing over their boots, Ian declared it a beautiful, magnificent day. Algernon did not argue. If he had recently been released from jail, found himself suddenly rich, and was enjoying the company of the lady he loved, he would have thought the day beautiful, too.

Ian's last obstacle was to get her brother's approval. It was obvious Darcy was appraising the young man closely, but not with a disapproving eye. Algernon was confident he would decide Ian had many excellent qualities, and he had certainly demonstrated strong character. He was also heir to a fine estate, a fact surely enhancing his suitability as a brother-in-law.

Darcy's acceptance of Ian Marshall was confirmed when he invited him to visit Pemberley in the spring. When publicly known, the invitation to Pemberley would remove any lingering cloud on Ian's character and reestablish his unquestioned place in society.

Shortly after the Darcys left Longbourn, Ian returned to Oakleigh, his childhood home. Algernon accompanied him to the door and was startled by an embrace. "Mr. Bennet, you are, and will always be, the best friend I ever had." Husky-voiced, he added, "God bless you."

Praise from Alexander Marshall, a kiss from Georgiana Darcy, and now gratitude and blessings from Ian.

Algernon was unnerved and made one of the most sincere prayers of his life: "Please, God, never let me emulate Sir William and arise every morning eager to do good deeds."

Chapter 32

Algernon did not forget his offer to draw Miss Pepper's likeness. When the Darcys were gone, he got to work. Although he usually did his sketching in the library, he decided to pose her in the dining hall by a window providing a serene winter background.

He spent almost every hour of the short winter days sketching her yet, despite her delight, was not at all satisfied when he was finished. She was actually more comely than he had portrayed, and he had not caught her alert expression. Perhaps, he had talked to her too much while he worked. He decided to wait until the days were longer and try again.

For her second portrait, he posed her sitting at the same window. This time the background show-ed the lively budding of spring. Her likeness was much better, but not quite right. He thought he might try a third time, instead of an ink drawing, perhaps an oil painting with a summer scene in the background.

He could not quite remember the conversation, but it seemed he had promised Miss Pepper to draw his own likeness. She had the servants carry down the full-length mirror from the upper hallway, and she positioned it exactly right for him to see himself while he sketched.

Drawing his own face, he worked quickly and carelessly, hardly caring how it turned out, and was a little embarrassed when he realized the face in the drawing was handsomer and definitely more youthful than the face in the mirror.

'I seem to have flattered myself unduly," he said.

Holding the finished work, Miss Pepper shook her head. "Not at all. It does not do you justice. Mr. Bennet, if I may say so, you are far better looking than this."

"Hmmm," he said noncommittally, afraid she would suspect her praise was pleasantly received. "If you will excuse me, I have letters to answer." He gestured toward a stack of correspondence.

He had received a letter from Jane when her last was still unanswered. She demanded, as much as her gentle nature could demand, that he visit soon to meet his grandson. Putting away his sketch pad, he answered her letters first, promising to make Bennet Bingley's acquaintance within the month. He was making arrangements for the journey when a letter arrived from the Wickhams, informing him he had a second grandchild. Baby Lydia had arrived.

"Lydia the third," Algernon mused. "If she is a true namesake, we had best prepare ourselves."

Algernon considered Mrs. Wickham's humble request for one of her sisters to be allowed a long visit to help while she adjusted to motherhood. He decided Kitty was too happily ensconced with the Bingleys, which made Mary the only daughter available. In addition, sending Mary would be safer. If Kitty went, Lydia would take it upon herself to find her a husband, and Lydia's husband-finding technique was alarming. Sister Mary was less likely to be persuaded away from her books and into man-hunting forays.

Joining Mary and Miss Pepper at the dinner table, Algernon announced the arrival of their new relative. After a round of congratulations, he added, "Lydia needs one of her sisters to help her. Mary, if you do not object, I would like you to go."

While Mary was composing her response, Algernon saw Miss Pepper's expression change. The smile that greeted news of little Lydia faded. She looked dismayed, then murmured, "Mary, I am certain you would find pleasure in helping your sister." After a moment, she added, "I have been very happy at Longbourn, but it is time for me to leave. Andrew has his assignment. Perhaps, if I go to Portsmouth, I can see him before he sails."

It had not occurred to Algernon, but certainly Miss Pepper would have to leave Longbourn if Mary did. He had forgotten to quell the rumors about them. Even if he had, she could hardly remain under his roof in the absence of the daughter for whom she was supposed to be a companion.

Setting her water goblet down, Mary said, "If my sister needs me, I will go and help her."

Algernon was not as surprised at Mary's simple statement as he would once have been. In recent weeks, she had often sounded rational, sometimes going whole days without uttering a single quote or sharing one wise and weighty thought. He credited Miss Pepper for the improvement. In return, he thought he should do something for her. She would be quite alone when her brother went to sea, and, despite feeling aghast by all the gratitude already heaped on him, he decided one more good deed would not ruin him.

At the Longs' ball, Mr. Allen had danced with her, and his visits to Longbourn were certainly more frequent than necessary. In fact, Algernon had been annoyed at the attention Mr. Allen paid Miss Pepper, often bringing her a supremely dull book or asking her help with an even duller sermon. The man had no right to intrude on her time, but if his attentions to the lady were serious, Algernon might be of assistance.

Although Ian Marshall would have been welcomed back to the parish with smiles and open arms, he no longer needed the position. Mr. Allen had acted as pastor for almost five months and done a creditable job. If his assignment were permanent, he would be in a position to take a wife. Mary would leave soon to join her sister. His own visit to the Bingleys could not be delayed. There was no time to waste, and as soon as he was up from the table, he went to talk to Mr. Allen.

Mr. Allen had boarded with relatives in Meryton and, with no place of his own, had eagerly accepted Algernon's offer of a temporary stay in the parsonage. He greeted his patron at the door and seemed such a happy man, it occurred to Algernon promoting his marriage might be an uncharitable act. Of course, Miss Pepper's company was not at all irksome. Her behavior would never embarrass him and teach him to prefer solitude. Indeed, she was a sensible woman, very clever at times, and rather comfortable to have around. If a man *wanted* to marry, she would be a superior choice.

Algernon told Mr. Allen his services met with approval and offered to make him parson. While

Mr. Allen was expressing his gratitude, Algernon casually perused his stack of books. Almanacs, several thick books of sermons, and a few uninteresting pamphlets—nothing else, not a single thing worth reading. Mr. Allen could not have a very lively mind and would be a boring companion. Algernon would have to tell Miss Pepper she could continue to use the library at Longbourn.

When Mr. Allen finished his tenth promise to work hard, Algernon brought up a more important issue. "Now that you are secured of an income, you will no doubt make plans for your future."

"Mr. Bennet. With your permission, the first thing I will do is add a room to the parsonage."

"In anticipation of a family, I daresay."

"True, my mother and sister can no longer stay with my aunt. If my position here is permanent, they can come to me."

"I see," Algernon said, concerned that Miss Pepper would not like two other women living in her home. He continued. "I am sure you will also be thinking about choosing a wife."

Mr. Allen's complexion flamed as red as his hair. "There is someone. Perhaps you are aware."

Algernon *was* aware and left, convinced Mr. Allen would be more than willing to marry Miss Pepper. He was in doubt about the lady's sentiments. Surely, she would want an intelligent hus-

band with a keen sense of discernment. Mr. Allen
was not quite a dullard, but he was hardly a match
for her. Of course, she could relieve the boredom of
the parsonage with frequent trips to the Longbourn
library, and they could still enjoy their lively con-
versations. At times, he might even ask her opinion
when making decisions. The decision to be made
now was for the lady alone.

When he entered the house, he was glad to hear
the pianoforte. With Mary playing away, Miss Pepper would be alone. He found her in the dining hall,
helping the maids rearrange a cabinet. He was about
to call her to the library, then decided he could
express himself better out-of-doors. "It is a lovely
evening and the early flowers are blooming," he
told her. "Perhaps you would enjoy a walk."

She hurried to get her bonnet and spencer, then
joined him at the door. As they made their way
down the path, Algernon said, "I think Mr. Allen
gave an excellent Easter sermon. What do you
think?"

"It was fine."

"He seems to be a very pleasant man."

The lady did not answer.

"I have made Mr. Allen's assignment permanent. He is now in a position to plan his future."

"Look," she said, pointing to a robin, "the first
one this year."

Algernon chuckled. "Most women would find his red hair unattractive."

She turned toward him. "I am very fond of red hair."

They strolled the stone path that twisted through the garden. It was warm for the season, and the air carried the aroma of spring. On impulse, Algernon stopped, carefully pinched off the stems of several jonquils in early bloom, and presented them to her. She carried the flowers in one hand and held his arm with the other.

They walked in silence for a few minutes, then he decided it was time. "My dear, Miss Pepper, what I am trying to say is this. I do not think you should go to Portsmouth. You are a fine woman. You have exceptional gifts and would be a splendid wife."

He was shocked when her hand slipped down his arm and crept into his.

"Algernon."

To his amazement, he felt his own hand close firmly over hers.

Chapter 33

Algernon could hardly tell the lady he was not the available bridegroom. She would be disappointed, perhaps broken-hearted, if she realized he had only been advancing the courtship of dull Mr. Allen. He could not inflict such regret, and his only course, as a benevolent, compassionate man, was to marry her.

To his surprise, the idea was not without appeal, and the marriage could not be delayed. Mary was leaving for Norfolk, and Miss Pepper could remain at Longbourn only by becoming Mrs. Bennet.

He wrote a letter to each daughter, never mentioning until the last paragraph that Miss Pepper and he were betrothed.

To his surprise, the information did not shock them as much as he had hoped. Strangely, Elizabeth's response suggested she had expected it:

Darcy and I are hardly surprised at the news of your engagement to dear Miss Pepper, and we wish both of you every joy.

Jane's letter of congratulations was still more baffling:

Dearest Father, Lizzy told me something was going on at Longbourn, and news of a wedding might be forthcoming. I am truly delighted and happy for you and look forward with joy to meeting Miss Pepper.

Puzzled, Algernon recalled Elizabeth and Darcy alluding to something "going on at Longbourn." Could they have detected something he missed? He felt strangely uneasy until deciding there had been nothing to detect. At the time, matrimonial thoughts had been as remote as the moon. He enjoyed a laugh thinking of how mistaken they had been.

Knowing her income might not provide for unexpected expenses, he offered to buy his bride a new gown for their wedding. She assured him it was unnecessary. By happy coincidence, she had almost finished sewing a gown she thought would do nicely. It was yellow, his favorite color.

His period of mourning for the first Mrs. Bennet was a bit abbreviated, a fact the neighborhood found most entertaining. The wittiest story was thought to be the one where Algernon paused at the altar to rip off his black ribbons.

Unfortunately, not everyone was entertained by his marriage. The Lucases were deeply distressed, and the unconfirmed report from Kent said Mr. Collins took to his bed. Their comfort was the assurance that, in the unlikely event the second Mrs. Bennet ventured into motherhood, Algernon Bennet had demonstrated he could not father a son.

Alas, before the first anniversary of the new Bennet union, a second Algernon Bennet entered the world. Baby Algernon had hardly outgrown his cradle when brother Andrew had need of it. Longbourn's trees were forever safe from Mr. Collins.

The Lucases, to their credit, did not give way to despair but, paying careful attention to the Bennet boys as they romped about, were often able to detect signs of their wasting away. More inspiring were the occasional happy reports of a contagious pestilence carrying off neighborhood children.

Their sisters were thrilled with the advent of little brothers and visited Longbourn often, allowing nieces, nephews, and cousins to know one another. Mr. and Mrs. Ian Marshall, the lady the former Miss Georgiana Darcy, were grateful to be included in the family circle. They loved Longbourn and were devoted to Algernon for making their union possible.

Algernon made the most of his second chance to be a good father and found unexpected joy in teaching and playing with his sons. He was strict but not too strict, and the only difficulty arose when he wanted them to sit still while he drew their pictures.

Dorinda, as he always called her to avoid confusing her with his first lady, made him a long, flowing shirt and a floppy hat to wear when he painted. At her urging, he began to display his work. Soon his paintings and drawings were in demand and began appearing in the homes of family and friends.

Occasionally, when outdoors sketching scenes of his beloved Longbourn, with his wife nearby reading, and two red-haired little boys playing on the lawn, he would be stricken with a mortifying thought. He, Algernon Bennet, squire of Longbourn, was a happily married man.

NICKOLAE GERSTNER began her freelance career writing magazine and newspaper articles. Her first book was an historical novel. She launched her mystery-writing career after listening to Mary Higgins Clark give the keynote address at a writers' conference. Her novels have been translated into many languages.

A native Chicagoan, she and her husband, John, now divide their time between homes in California and New York. She is pictured at Austen's grave in Winchester Cathedral in England.

Only copy in my system